"Not many m[obscured] demands of [obscured] maybe anoth[obscured]

"Or a cop," Carrie said.

"I can't believe we're having this conversation," Kelly replied. "Trust me, there is absolutely no chance of a relationship between Cole and me. None. Zip. *Nada.*"

Carrie grinned. "But you have to admit he's a hunk."

"Really? I hadn't noticed."

"Li-ar," Carrie singsonged.

Kelly only smiled, and they parted company.

Oh, she'd noticed that Cole Younger Outlaw was a hunk. Every female hormone in her body was on red alert. She glanced toward him and found him watching her.

He winked.

Good Lord, could he read her mind?

Dear Reader,

This is the last of three stories about the Outlaw brothers, *The Sheriff*, *The Judge* and now *The Cop*, all from a family traditionally named for famous outlaws and all in law enforcement and public service. When I was creating Cole Younger Outlaw's story, I first considered setting it in Houston—logical, since the oldest son had been in HPD homicide for many years—but the colorful characters in the small town of Naconiche (NAK-uh-KNEE-chee) had grown on me. To prove that good things can come of terrible incidents, I brought Cole back to his hometown to recuperate from his serious injury...and to find a whole new life in the place of his roots.

Now, there's no real town named Naconiche—and, no, it's not patterned after Nacogdoches, the historical small town where I lived for many years—but there is a Naconiche Creek in East Texas, and I liked the sound of the Indian word. The Outlaws' hometown is a composite of many places in the heart of the Piney Woods where my ancestors lived when Texas was still a republic.

Naconiche and the Twilight Inn seem to be magical places, and with one gorgeous redhead thrown into the mix, the cynical and battle-scarred cop is about to be turned every which way but loose. I had fun writing about the sassy Dr. Kelly Martin and the tough Cole Outlaw, and I can promise that you're in for lots of love and laughter! Join me and see if I'm not right.

Visit me at www.eclectics.com/JanHudson.

Jan Hudson

THE COP
Jan Hudson

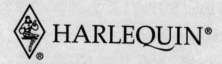

HARLEQUIN®

TORONTO • NEW YORK • LONDON
AMSTERDAM • PARIS • SYDNEY • HAMBURG
STOCKHOLM • ATHENS • TOKYO • MILAN • MADRID
PRAGUE • WARSAW • BUDAPEST • AUCKLAND

ISBN 0-373-75029-3

THE COP

Copyright © 2004 by Janece Hudson.

All rights reserved. Except for use in any review, the reproduction or utilization of this work in whole or in part in any form by any electronic, mechanical or other means, now known or hereafter invented, including xerography, photocopying and recording, or in any information storage or retrieval system, is forbidden without the written permission of the publisher, Harlequin Enterprises Limited, 225 Duncan Mill Road, Don Mills, Ontario, Canada M3B 3K9.

All characters in this book have no existence outside the imagination of the author and have no relation whatsoever to anyone bearing the same name or names. They are not even distantly inspired by any individual known or unknown to the author, and all incidents are pure invention.

This edition published by arrangement with Harlequin Books S.A.

® and TM are trademarks of the publisher. Trademarks indicated with ® are registered in the United States Patent and Trademark Office, the Canadian Trade Marks Office and in other countries.

www.eHarlequin.com

Printed in U.S.A.

For Karen Solem, Agent Extraordinaire

And with special thanks to Sherry Wallace,
Hospice of Deep East Texas
and Greg Sowell,
Nacogdoches Police Department

Chapter One

"Pull off your pants and lie down," she repeated.

Cole Younger Outlaw turned from the bedroom window, and his eyes swept her with a slow, clothes-stripping scrutiny that sucked the air from her lungs. One corner of his mouth twitched upward. "Tell you what, Red," he said in a low rumble that sent an acre of goose bumps racing over her skin. "I'll pull off my pants if you'll pull off yours."

For a nanosecond she actually considered taking him up on the offer. He was without a doubt the most...phenomenal man she'd ever encountered. Even in ragged sweats and with several days' growth of dark beard, sex appeal oozed from his pores and wafted across the room like nitrous oxide. Hard. Dangerous. Survival instincts would have sent a lesser woman screaming from the room, which, she was sure, was what he intended.

She was made of sterner stuff.

"That's not an option, Mr. Outlaw. And please don't call me Red. My name is Kelly Martin. *Dr.* Kelly Martin."

His dark brows lifted a tad, and he gave her another

slow perusal. "You sure don't look like any doctor I've seen lately." He flashed a full-fledged grin, and her knees almost buckled. "The offer still holds."

"Look, Mr. Outlaw—"

"Call me Cole, darlin'."

She ignored the "darlin'" part. "Look, Cole, I have an office full of patients waiting, and I don't have time for games. Dr. Ware is in surgery all day, and I'm here as a favor to your mother. She and your dad are worried sick about you, and so are your brothers. You've holed up in this room and refused to go to physical therapy. You won't cooperate with anybody who's trying to help you. You haven't—"

"Put a sock in it, Red." He scowled and turned back to the window which was festooned with a bright holiday swag.

Kelly was torn between clobbering him with her medical bag and stalking from the room. Instead she tossed the bag and her jacket on the bed and walked closer to him. "Exactly what is your problem?"

"My problem?" He glared at her with storm-cloud gray eyes. "Besides losing a chunk of lung, getting my hip and leg shot all to hell and being a cripple the rest of my life, you mean?"

She waited only two beats before she shot him a cheeky grin. "Yeah, besides that, flatfoot."

He ducked his head, but not before Kelly saw a hint of a smile. When he looked up a few seconds later, he was scowling again. "I'm not a flatfoot. I'm a cop. *Was* a cop."

"You can be a cop again—if you'll go to therapy."

"Sorry, Red, it won't wash. There's no way in hell

I can work homicide again, and I'm not cut out for being a desk jockey. You got a cigarette on you?''

Kelly patted all her pockets. "Nope. Fresh out." She fished a small sucker from her purple lab coat. "This is the best I can do." When he reached for it, she popped it back into her pocket. "The examination comes first. Take off your pants."

"Don't try to play games with me, Red," he growled. "I eat little gals like you for lunch."

Kelly burst into laughter. His scowl only deepened. "Try it," she said, then deepened her voice to add in her best Dirty Harry imitation, "Make...my...day."

She thought the corner of his mouth twitched upward again, but she couldn't be sure because he suddenly hooked his thumbs in the waistband of his faded sweats and stripped them off. Next the shirt landed on the floor beside the pants, and he turned to her. "Examine away."

Her woman's breath caught for less than a heartbeat before the physician kicked in. "I see the incisions seem to be healing nicely. Let me get my gear." She retrieved her bag from the bed and took out her stethoscope. Automatically she held the diaphragm in her fist and blew on the metal, warming it before she placed it on his chest. "Take a deep breath."

After listening to his heart and lungs, she carefully checked the surgical sites and damage to his chest and back. The scar from the exit wound was more vicious than the one from the surgeon's scalpel. She knew that things had been touch-and-go with him for several days after he was shot and that he had spent weeks in a Houston hospital before his folks had brought him back home with them to finish recuperating. Naconiche was a small town, and everybody had known about his gun battle with a murder suspect. Too, she shared an office suite with Noah Ware, the surgeon who was Cole's local doctor.

When the time came to check his left hip and leg, Kelly pulled up a nearby straight chair and sat down to examine the places.

"Ugly looking mess, isn't it?" Cole asked.

"I've seen much worse. I worked in Ben Taub ER in Houston for a year. I saw more gunshot wounds than most doctors see in a lifetime. Bet this hurt like a son of a gun," she said as she gently probed the sites, which were now patched with pins. Kelly asked him to move and bend, then walk a few steps.

He had to use his walker and limped badly.

"Your injuries are healing properly, but it's imperative that you go to physical therapy daily," Kelly said. "I can't find any reason to contraindicate PT, and it will do wonders for your recovery."

"Sure you haven't got a cigarette?"

She took a patch from her bag, peeled off the back and slapped it on his right hip.

"What's that?"

"A nicotine patch. I'll have the drugstore deliver some more. You're not to smoke a cigarette under any circumstance, and don't pester your folks to buy any for you." She retrieved the sugar-free lollipop from her pocket. "Suck on this. It'll help some."

He scowled at the smiley face on the plastic-wrapped candy. "Like hell it will."

She glanced at her watch. "Okay, hardcase, I have to get back to my office, and you need to keep your PT appointment at the hospital."

"No."

"*No?* For goodness' sakes, why not?"

He glared at her for several seconds, but she didn't so much as blink. Finally he turned away and mumbled something.

"Say again."

"I said I can't get down the damned stairs, and I'm not going to have my brothers carry me down like a baby."

Pride. Big time. She nodded. "I understand."

"I should have never given in to my folks and come here. I should have stayed in Houston. Mama's hovering is driving me nuts."

And his recalcitrance was driving his mother nuts. She nodded again. "I'll work on a solution, Cole. You can get dressed now."

He glanced down at his nakedness. "Bother you, Red?"

"Nope. But you might look a little better if you'd shave." With that perfect exit line, she turned and walked from the room.

"Red," he called after her.

She stopped at the door.

"Forget something?"

Kelly turned and saw Cole standing there, still naked, with her medical bag dangling from his fingers.

She stalked back, grabbed her bag and hurried out. His laughter followed her as she clattered down the stairs.

Miss Nonie, Cole's mother, waited for her at the foot of the stairs that ended in the back of the Double Dip ice-cream parlor. Nonie and Wes Outlaw lived in the apartment upstairs from the business that Nonie had run since she retired from teaching and Wes retired as sheriff of the East Texas county. Two or three years before, the couple had divided their extensive ranch property among their five children, leaving their big house to their son Frank and his twins, and moved into town.

Miss Nonie looked worried. "How is he, Dr. Kelly?"

Kelly patted Nonie's back. "He's doing very well considering what he's been through. He simply needs time and physical therapy."

"But he refuses to go to physical therapy. His father and I have talked to him. His brothers have tried to talk to him. He won't listen to any of us, and we're all at our wit's end."

Kelly smiled. "He *is* a little hardheaded. Let me work on an idea that I have, and I'll get back to you later today. How about an ice-cream cone for the road? Butter pecan would be good."

Between the ice cream and leaving her coat in Cole's room, Kelly nearly froze before she got to her car. An early December norther had blown through the day before, and the morning temperatures were in the forties. But she'd sooner be switched with a peach limb than go back for her jacket. She'd pick it up later.

COLE STOOD at the window and watched Kelly Martin drive away. Now *there* was a woman. And a *doctor* of all things. Tall, long-legged and gorgeous. Any man would give a month's pay to have that curly tumble of red hair spread across his pillow. With those snapping green eyes and kiss-me lips, she revved his motors more than any female he'd run across in years—for all the good it did him now. Hell, he couldn't even dress himself without breaking out in a sweat.

He snagged his clothes from the floor and hobbled the few steps to his bed. Sure enough, by the time he'd pulled on the pants and shirt he was breathing hard and dripping wet. He wasn't any use to himself or anybody else like he was. If he hadn't been so doped up on painkillers, he would never have agreed to come to Naconiche.

Of course, his apartment in Houston was on the third floor, but he could have made out with pizza delivery and a few groceries from one of those online places. Here, he was worried about his mother. She ran up and down those stairs a dozen times a day checking on him, and she was no spring chicken anymore. Cole thought again about taking his brother Frank up on his offer to stay with the twins and him, but he didn't want to impose, especially now that Frank was engaged. J.J.'s place was out—stairs again—and he was engaged, too. In fact, J.J. and Mary Beth were getting married in a few days. They had plenty going on without having to worry about their gimpy brother.

Nope, that wasn't an option.

Hell, he knew he needed to go to PT. The sooner he got able to tend to himself, the sooner he could be out of everybody's hair. Cole wasn't used to being dependent on anybody, and he didn't like being helpless. Not a damned bit.

He was just going to have to try to get down those stairs by himself.

KELLY DROPPED BY the Twilight Tearoom at the end
of the lunch hour and had a quick bite as she sometimes did when she had time. In the odd spare moments she'd had since she'd seen Cole Outlaw that
morning, thoughts of him had preyed on her mind. In
some ways he looked very much like his brothers, J.J.
and Frank, both patients of hers. Tall, dark, handsome. But life had carved a different character into
his features, his bearing—and she found him stun-
ningly seductive. Odd, since she'd never had such
feelings about a patient before—not that he was actually her patient.

Of course she'd noticed that his brothers were
good-looking guys, but being around them had never
assaulted her senses and jolted her libido. The family
patriarch, old Judge John Outlaw, thought naming his
sons for notorious characters was politically smart—
they'd have a leg up on opponents or in business. The
tradition had continued through his grandsons. Of all
the current crop of Outlaws named for famous des-
perados, Cole Younger Outlaw came closest to living
up to his name. He might have been a cop, but he
was as menacing as any gunslinger who ever lived.
And, she admitted, turned her on like crazy. Interesting. Very interesting. She wasn't sure if she wanted
to pursue these unusual feelings or not.

When Kelly finished her chicken quesadillas, the
tables were almost empty, and she went back into the
kitchen to talk with Mary Beth Parker. Mary Beth
owned the tearoom and the adjacent Twilight Inn, a
small motel she had restored. She and J. J. Outlaw,
the current county sheriff, were getting married on
Saturday.

"Got a second?" Kelly asked as she stuck her head in.

"Sure," Mary Beth said, wiping her hands and coming to the door. "What's up?"

"Do you have a vacancy at the inn?" she asked quietly.

Mary Beth grinned. "Need a place for a rendez-vous?"

Kelly rolled her eyes at her friend and patient. "I wish. No, I'm trying to find a place for Cole to stay while he recuperates."

"I thought he was staying with Miss Nonie and Wes."

"He is, but he needs to be on the ground floor...and he needs a place where he feels some independence but where his family could drop in with casseroles occasionally. The inn would be ideal. And I thought that since he's family...well, that the cost wouldn't be too prohibitive."

"That wouldn't be a problem, but we're full. Besides our regular guests, tomorrow I'm expecting out-of-town friends for the wedding."

Kelly sighed. "So much for that."

"Wait a minute. I may have another solution."

When Mary Beth told her the idea, Kelly grinned. "Perfect. Can you talk to him this afternoon? And maybe it would be best to present the notion to him in a...delicate way."

"The male ego thing, you mean?"

"Exactly."

"Gotcha."

COLE HADN'T MADE IT past the third step when he had to sit down on the stairs and catch his breath.

Three steps was one better than he'd done that morning. Shaking and sweating from his effort, he muttered a string of oaths that would have shocked his mother if she'd heard them. He felt as useless as hip pockets on a hog.

After resting several minutes, he was about ready to try again when he saw J.J. and Mary Beth coming upstairs.

"Hey, big brother," J.J. said. "Whatcha doing sitting out here?"

"Waiting for a bus," Cole said.

"Need any help?"

"Nope."

"Mary Beth wants to ask you something."

"Ask away."

"It's a big favor," Mary Beth said, "and if you don't feel up to it, just say so. I have a problem. You know that I own the Twilight Inn and Tearoom."

She looked as nervous as a long-tailed cat in a roomful of rocking chairs, and Cole tried not to grin at his future sister-in-law, a pretty blonde who J.J. had been crazy about since they were kids. "Yes. Heard that you inherited it and fixed it up."

"Right. It was a mess. The problem now is that Katy and I—you know my daughter, Katy?"

He smiled. "The little blond imp who wanted to see my bullet holes."

"Yes, sorry about that, Cole. Anyhow, Katy and I are moving from the manager's apartment to the new house. We're trying to get settled before the wedding, but the person who was supposed to move in and take over as night manager has backed out, and I'm in a predicament. I was wondering if—oh, no, forget it. It's too much of an imposition.''

"What is?" Cole asked.

"She was hoping that you might be able to fill in for a few weeks," J.J. said.

"Just till after the Christmas holidays," Mary Beth said. "I'm sure I can find another college student then who'll take over the job for room and board. But you're probably not up to it yet, Cole. It was a crazy idea. I'm sorry I mentioned it.''

"Whoa, darlin'," Cole said. "What does a night manager have to do?"

"Not a lot, actually," Mary Beth said. "Answer the phone in the evening and check in an occasional traveler who rings the bell for a room at night. You don't even have to stay up. Basically just be there for security and to handle emergencies. The only emergency we've had was when the toilet overflowed in Unit Three. I had to call the plumber at midnight. The domino bunch takes care of the day shift.''

"The domino bunch?"

"Four old geezers who work around the motel for lunch and a place to play dominoes," J.J. said. "I imagine you know all of them."

Cole was naturally suspicious, but he didn't care if it was a put-up job or not. Mary Beth's offer sounded like an answer to his prayers. "I'll be your temporary night manager."

"Are you sure you feel like it?" Mary Beth asked.

"I'm sure."

Mary Beth knelt on the stairs and threw her arms around Cole. "Oh, thank you, thank you, thank you," she said, planting kisses on his face.

"Hey, there," J.J. grumbled, "that's enough of that."

Cole laughed for the second time that day. "When do I start?"

Chapter Two

Shortly after lunch Kelly tapped on Cole's bedroom door. The biggest and burliest of the hospital's physical therapists stood behind her with a wheelchair.

When the door opened, Cole scowled at her. "What are you doing here?"

He still hadn't shaved, and he had on well-worn gray sweats that looked even worse than the ones he'd worn the day before. On his feet were a pair of fleece-lined moccasins that looked like something his mother might have bought him—or that Wes had received for Christmas sometime.

"We've come to move you to your new digs," Kelly said, smiling brightly. "Are you packed?"

He glanced to a black duffel bag on the bed. "Not much to pack, but I've been ready since daylight. My brothers are supposed to come by when Frank gets out of court."

He frowned at the therapist. "Who are you?"

"Dan Robert Thurston, sir." The therapist offered his hand, and Cole shook it. "Thought I'd give you a ride down." He motioned to the wheelchair. "Hop in and buckle up."

"Down the stairs? In that?"

"Dan Robert's a pro. It's a piece of cake for him," Kelly said. "Not only is he a physical therapist, he's a weight lifter."

Cole didn't look convinced, but he shrugged and sat in the lightweight chair. Dan Robert strapped him in while Kelly collected the duffel and the walker from Cole's room. In a couple of minutes, they were downstairs.

"You make this seem easy," Cole said.

"It is easy," Dan Robert said, "with a little experience. It's more a matter of leverage than muscle. Shoot, they even got machines now that you can attach to wheelchairs and climb stairs by yourself."

"Why haven't I heard about them?" Cole asked.

Kelly grinned. "It's the sort of information you get if you're in physical therapy." She ignored his rude snort.

Miss Nonie bustled over as they passed through the shop. "Are you sure you'll be all right alone, son?"

"I'll be fine, Mom."

"Your dad and I will be over tonight with your supper. Is there anything else you need?"

"Not a thing," Cole said. "And don't worry about my supper. I'll order a pizza or something."

"But—"

"Don't worry about it, Miss Nonie," Kelly said. "Mary Beth plans to leave a plate from lunch in the fridge. He won't starve." She waved as they went outside and loaded into her car, Cole in the passenger seat and Dan Robert in the back.

When she pulled away and turned left, Cole said,

"Aren't we going the wrong way to the Twilight Inn?"

"Nope. I have to drop Dan Robert by the hospital, and we thought while we were there that you could go in with him and have your physical therapy session."

Cole cocked an eyebrow at her. "Who is *we?*"

"Think of it as the imperial 'we,'" she said with a flutter of her hand. After a few moments of silence, she said, "What? No argument?"

He shrugged. "Would it do any good?"

"Not a bit."

Dan Robert made a slight choking sound from the back seat.

When they stopped at the hospital entrance, Kelly said to Cole, "I'll pick you up here in an hour."

"Don't you have patients to see?"

"It's my afternoon off. I'll...be...back."

Cole started to say something, then clamped his mouth shut. She could see his molars getting a workout.

COLE HAD BEEN RIGHT, Kelly thought. He hadn't had much to pack. In the duffel she found the sweats from the day before, four pairs of pajamas, a robe, some ratty underwear and three pairs of white and two pairs of gray socks. Besides his shaving kit, two paperback novels—and her forgotten jacket of all things—that was it. Why did he have her jacket in his bag?

She shrugged and checked the sizes of his few belongings. Obviously the man needed some clothes. At least some more sweats to knock around in. Easy on and easy off, they would be simple to manage.

By the time she drove to the hospital door an hour later, she'd been able to do a fair amount of shopping. Dan Robert was just wheeling Cole out the door as she pulled up. Cole looked exhausted.

"Tired?" she asked when he was settled in the front seat.

He merely nodded.

By the time they reached the Twilight Inn, he was sound asleep. He looked so peaceful that she hated to wake him, so she sat in front of the manager's apartment and let him sleep.

B.D., one of the four old fellows who worked at the motel and played dominoes in the office, came outside to check. Kelly held her fingers to her lips and shook her head, and he ducked back inside.

While Cole slept, she studied him. In the way that sleep softens features, his had modified to more a boyish cast, but he still looked far from innocent. He was a handsome man, but he reminded her more of a battle-scarred gladiator than a romantic Lancelot. The creases bisecting his forehead, though relaxed, were permanently etched there, and his jaw was clenched—probably a permanent state, as well.

An old scar carved a crescent on his left cheekbone, and another furrowed through his beard at his chin. His nose looked as if it had been rearranged a couple of times, and a lone pockmark faintly pitted his cheek an inch below the thick, dark sweep of lashes. The scar was probably the result of childhood chicken pox or adolescent acne, and it made him somehow seem more…vulnerable. Well, maybe not vulnerable.

The whole package that was Cole Outlaw made her toes curl and her fingers itch to run themselves through the waves of his thick hair and over the planes of his face and—

She squirmed in the seat and turned her attention to a mockingbird sitting on a power line. What was with her? Good Lord, she felt as giddy as a high school girl.

After about twenty minutes, Kelly gently shook Cole awake.

He sat up with a start, instantly alert and scowling.

"We're home," she announced in her perkiest voice.

"Home?"

"The Twilight Inn."

"The old place looks a lot different from the last time I saw it."

"Which was?"

"Oh, I don't know," he said. "Maybe five, ten years ago. It was a dump."

"It was boarded up and falling down when Mary Beth started renovations last spring. A lot of folks pitched in and helped. Now it's a charming little motel," she said, motioning to the row of neatly painted units with yellow chrysanthemums still blooming in the window boxes. "And the restaurant has been refurbished as well. Mary Beth serves the best lunch in town."

"No breakfast or dinner?"

"Nope," she said, "but I bought some breakfast items at the grocery store, and one of the guys will bring you an extra meal at lunch to stash in the fridge for dinner."

She hopped out and got the wheelchair from the

trunk. By the time she got to the passenger door, Cole was struggling to get out.

When he saw her with the chair, he waved her away. "If you'll hand me my walker, I can make it in."

"Humor me this time and let me push."

He started to argue, then clamped his mouth shut and sat down in the wheelchair. They hadn't gone three steps when the office door opened and the four old guys spilled out.

"Land sakes," one of them said, sticking out his hand to Cole. "I haven't seen you in a coon's age. Bet you don't remember me."

"I sure do, Howard, but it looks like you've lost a little more on top."

Howard cackled and ran his hand over a head covered only by a few liver spots and a pink patch or two. "That's for sure. Then you probably remember B.D. and Curtis and Will here."

After Cole shook hands with all the men, Will said, "Need some help getting in?"

"I have some things in the back seat and in the trunk," Kelly said.

"You supervise the unloading," B.D. told Kelly, "and I'll roll Cole inside." B.D. was wisp thin and looked as if a powder puff could knock him over. When Cole appeared concerned about the prospect of an eightysomething guy pushing him, the old fellow must have caught the wary expression. He patted Cole's shoulder and said, "Don't you worry none, son. I've handled one of these contraptions more times than you can shake a stick at."

He proceeded to expertly wheel Cole into the office

unit while the other domino players brought the rest of the items from Kelly's car.

The apartment behind the office was more like a small suite: two rooms, one with a kitchenette in the corner, and a bathroom. The main room, which had been Mary Beth's, held only a few pieces of furniture including a sofa and a large leather recliner. Cole settled in the recliner, and Kelly stood his walker next to it.

"There you go," Howard said, setting the last of the grocery bags on a small table in the kitchen corner. "We'll get on about our game. You need anything, Cole, just give a holler."

"I'll do it, Howard. Thank you."

"You might have to holler twice," Will said with a wink. "Couple of us are a mite hard of hearing."

"He don't have to holler," Curtis said. "All he has to do is push that little button right there." Curtis pointed out the intercom on the phone base beside Cole.

After the old fellows said their goodbyes and left, Kelly took off her sweater and draped it over the back of a chair in the kitchen nook. She stowed the perishables in the small fridge and the other groceries in a cabinet under the microwave, listing the items to Cole as she worked.

"You should have plenty for a simple breakfast and for snacks." She picked up another large shopping bag. "And I bought you some new sweats and things—without holes." She grinned.

He glanced down at his shirt where the "HPD PIGS" across the chest was faded almost to oblivion. "You don't like my football outfit?"

"It's charming, but I think it's nearing retirement." She stashed the new clothes in the chest by the bathroom door. "Your pajamas are in the top drawer here."

"I don't wear pajamas."

Her heart tripped. She didn't dare look at him. "You have several pair."

"My mom bought them."

"Oh." She closed the drawer and turned. Playing perky again, she said, "Let's see. The bedroom is through there. The bathroom is here. I put your shaving kit on the counter. The fridge and the microwave and the coffeepot are over there. The remote for the TV is on the table beside you with the phone. I guess that about covers it." Why was she babbling? She took a deep breath. "Want something to drink?"

"Yeah. A beer would be nice."

"Sorry. No beer with the medication you're on. You may have Coke, cream soda, milk, orange juice, apple juice, tomato juice or water. Or coffee. And Mary Beth left a big plate of brownies."

"A cup of coffee would taste good. And the whole plate of brownies. Join me?"

"Only if I can have two brownies," she said as she poured water into the coffeemaker. "I'm a sucker for chocolate."

"I'll arm wrestle you for them."

She laughed. "Don't look so smug. I'm stronger than I look. I could probably take you two out of three."

His playfulness vanished. "In the condition I'm in, I wouldn't be surprised."

Fighting the urge to sigh, Kelly said, "Don't use

that as an excuse, buster. I could probably take you on your best day.''

There was a flicker at the corner of his mouth. ''Okay. I'll let you have a brownie.''

''Two.''

''Okay, two. I'm easy.''

She doubted that. Her instincts told her that nothing about Cole Outlaw was easy. While the coffee dripped, Kelly curled up on the couch. ''How did the therapy go?''

Cole shrugged. He shrugged a lot. He didn't seem to be much of a talker.

''Your dad said that either he or one of the domino guys will drive you to your appointments.''

''He told me. You're not from around here are you, Red?''

She shook her head. ''I'm originally from Dallas. And my name is *Kelly.*''

''How'd you get from Dallas to Naconiche?''

''I drove.''

Cole let out a short bark of laughter. ''Let me re-phrase that…Kelly. What happened between the time you were a kid in Dallas and your arriving in Naconiche as a doctor?''

''You want the long version or the short?''

''Let's start with the short, and we'll flesh it out later.''

''Well, I grew up in Dallas.''

''Big family?''

''I had a younger sister, but she died when I was in junior high. Leukemia.''

''Parents?''

''One of each,'' she said. ''My mom is president

of a bank, and my dad is a biology professor at SMU.''

His eyebrows went up. "Interesting. Did you go to SMU?''

"Nope. I went to the University of Texas. Your brother Frank's fiancée and I were sorority sisters there. How about you?''

"I never joined a sorority.''

Kelly smiled. "I meant where did you go to school?''

"Sam Houston in Huntsville. It has the best criminal justice department in the state. Why did you decide to become a doctor?''

"I'm not sure. Probably because I was always good at science, and I wanted to help people. Maybe losing my little sister had something to do with it.'' She got up and poured coffee and brought the brownies over to where they were sitting. "Why did you become a cop?''

"It's in the genes. All the Outlaws are cops of one sort or another.''

"I haven't read anything in the research that suggests career choice is genetic.'' She polished off her first brownie and reached for another. "These are good. Mary Beth is a great cook.''

"Yep. J.J.'s a lucky man. How did you get from sorority girl to doctor to here?''

"I went to medical school in Houston and did my internship and residency there and stayed on to work for a while. I learned that one of the doctors in Naconiche was retiring, and I applied to work with him and take his place. And here I am.''

"You never married?"

"Nope. I never had time. You?"

"Once. It didn't take. I learned I'm not the marrying kind."

For some reason Kelly's heart sank, which was silly. She barely knew the man. And as soon as he was rehabilitated, he'd go back to Houston. Nothing about him indicated that he was a candidate for a relationship. Still, she had a mighty urge to swan dive into those marvelous, mysterious eyes.

She stood. "I've got to run. You need to rest, and I have to check on a couple of patients at the hospital. Need anything before I go?"

"Not a thing. Say, I want to pay you for the stuff you bought, but I don't have any money or a checkbook. You take a credit card?"

She laughed. "Don't worry about it. I charged the clothes to you at Olsen's, and the groceries are on me."

"Thanks, Red."

"Kelly."

"Kelly. Come back and visit sometime."

"I will."

"Is that a promise?"

"It's a promise."

As soon as she left Kelly realized that she'd left her sweater behind. Oh, blast it! Now both her jacket and her sweater were there. Freudian slip? An excuse to return? Maybe. Cole was an intriguing man, and she couldn't deny that she was affected by him. She would drop by tomorrow night after aerobics class and pick up her forgotten items.

COLE DECIDED he wanted another cup of coffee, but he quickly learned that he couldn't carry a full mug and navigate with it and the walker back to the recliner. He cursed and drank the coffee standing up. When he finished he noticed the brown sweater hanging on the back of the straight chair.

He picked the soft garment up and sniffed it. A faint scent of spices and field flowers. The material smelled of her—just like the jacket she'd left behind. He hung the sweater over his walker and moved back to his recliner to sit down. Wadding the sweater in both hands, he buried his face in it and breathed deeply. He was bone tired, but not too tired to imagine what it would feel like to have the woman under the fabric. He felt himself stir.

Oh, hell! he thought, disgusted with his behavior. Now that he was a cripple, he was turning into one of those perverts who got off on fetishes. He started to throw the sweater across the room, but he couldn't quite make himself let go. He dropped it across his lap and reached for another brownie.

Chapter Three

He'd learned a lot in the past twenty-four hours, Cole thought as he poured coffee into the Thermos. Mostly tips from Dan Robert during his therapy session. Now he had snap-on bags and a basket on his walker that reminded him of the gear on his bike when he was a kid. He stuck the Thermos in one of the side pockets, a mug into another and made it back to his chair without worrying about spills.

B.D. and Curtis had driven him to the hospital that afternoon, and his dad had picked him up. He'd been too tired to talk much with his dad. In fact, he'd fallen asleep soon after they returned to the motel. He hadn't awakened until J.J. stopped by about five. He hadn't stayed long.

Sometime later, the doorbell rang, and Cole opened the door between the apartment and the office. He smiled when he saw Kelly Martin standing there in a bright green sweat suit, her hair wadded on top of her head and held by a big yellow clip.

''You look like a leprechaun.''

She grinned. ''Leprechauns are wee folks. At close to six feet, I'm more like the Jolly Green Giant.''

"You're not six feet tall."

"Near enough. I'm almost five-ten."

"That's two inches, and two inches can make a world of difference."

She raised her eyebrows, an amused expression on her face. "Really?"

"Yep. If that bullet in my chest had been two inches over, I'd be dead."

"And if you'd been wearing a protective vest, you wouldn't have had more than a bruise."

"I wasn't planning on a shoot-out."

She touched his face and ran her fingers lightly along his jaw. "You've shaved."

"Yeah. This morning. Want a cup of coffee?"

"Thanks, but I don't have time. I'm on my way to aerobics class next door. I hope we don't disturb you. The music can get pretty loud."

"I'll manage."

"Do you need anything?" she asked.

"Not a thing. Maybe you can stop by after your class. I have a couple of those brownies left."

"Don't tempt me. I wish I could, but I have to make rounds at the hospital."

"Some other time then."

"It's a deal. See you later." With a flutter of her fingers, she was gone.

He stood there for a few minutes after she left, feeling funny. Uplifted, he thought, trying to put a word to his feelings. No, that was dumb. Sounded like a spiritual experience in a tent revival.

He pushed his walker back to the recliner, eased into the seat and sat there for a minute, the backs of his fingers absently brushing his jaw. Then he dry washed his face with his hands and turned on an old *Gunsmoke* rerun.

KELLY WAS STRIPPING down to her exercise shorts when the door to Unit 2 opened. She glanced up toward the new arrival and was delighted to see the dark-haired woman who entered. "Hey, Carrie! When did you get into town?"

"This afternoon."

"And you're in exercise class instead of with your fiancée?"

Carrie Campbell, an old sorority sister from UT days and newfound friend, was engaged to Judge Frank Outlaw. She was a landman for an oil company and finishing up some projects before she moved to Naconiche and set up a law practice.

"Frank wanted to talk with his brother Cole, so I thought I'd drop by and sweat with the gang for a few minutes," Carrie said, smiling and waving to some of the other women gathered. "I'm going over to meet Cole after Frank has time to use his persuasive skills."

"His persuasive skills?"

"Yep. Seems that Cole has announced that he isn't going to J.J. and Mary Beth's wedding."

"For heaven's sake, why not?" Kelly asked.

"Search me. I think J.J.'s feelings are hurt, and Miss Nonie's beside herself. Frank's going to, quote, 'try to talk some sense into him.'"

Mary Beth Parker, soon to be Outlaw, hurried in. "Sorry I'm late, gang, but it seems as if I have a million things to do. Wanted to remind you that I won't be here next week." She grinned. "We'll be on our honeymoon, but Beverly will take over the class for me while I'm gone. Bev, will you get the music?"

"Listen, my friend," Carrie said to Kelly as they lined up, "I'm going to be swamped with all the family doings tomorrow, but I'll see you at the wedding on Saturday. I'm eager to catch up on all the latest."

"Great."

KELLY GOT A BEEP from the hospital about the time the exercise class was over. One of her patients was having problems, so instead of going home to shower and change first, she headed immediately to Naconiche Memorial.

She knew she was in trouble when she spotted Warren Iverson and his wife at the nurses' station. The moment Mr. Iverson caught sight of her in sweats and damp hair, his beady eyes popped, and his bulldog jowls began to quiver. Mrs. Iverson stood beside him like a cornered mouse. Warren Iverson was one of the few human beings on Earth who she could actually say she detested. Unfortunately he was the chairman of the hospital board. And to put it mildly, she wasn't on his Christmas card list, either.

He looked her up and down as if she were a fresh pile he'd just stepped in. "Dr. Martin!"

She forced a bit of a smile with her curt nod. "Mr. Iverson. Mrs. Iverson."

"I can't believe that you're in the hospital dressed like that!"

Biting her lip to hold back a stinging reply, she simply shrugged and stepped around him to get her patient's chart and speak with the nurse. Bedamned if she was going to make excuses to that jerk, nor was she going to be goaded into creating a scene. He would love an excuse to yank her hospital privileges.

Watching him from the corner of her eye, Kelly saw his mouth working like a hooked catfish and steeled herself for another assault. Thankfully it didn't come. Mrs. Iverson timidly tugged at his coat sleeve, and he stalked down the hall.

Lorene Cuthbert, the middle-aged R.N. at the station, glared after Iverson. "Sanctimonious old fart!" she muttered as she and Kelly went in the opposite direction. "What does he have against you anyhow?"

Kelly chuckled. "Maybe he doesn't like red-heads."

But that wasn't what he had against her. Kelly knew exactly why Warren Iverson hated her. He had found the birth control pills that Kelly had prescribed for his daughter Rachel. Forget that Rachel was eighteen. Forget that she was sleeping with most of the single men in town and a few of the married ones. Forget that Kelly had talked with her repeatedly about the physical dangers of her behavior. Iverson had found the pills and gone into a rage, calling Rachel a whore and calling Kelly worse. When his daughter turned up pregnant a few months later, he threw her out of the house and blamed everything on Kelly for encouraging such abominable and licentious behavior.

Kelly shook off the effects of her encounter with him and put on a pleasant face for her patient.

Mrs. Phelps, an eighty-seven-year-old widow, smiled sweetly as they entered her room. "Now, don't you look pretty in green?"

"Why, thank you," Kelly said. "I hope I don't smell like a horse. I've been to aerobics class."

"With Mary Beth? I liked going to her seniors stretching class when I felt up to it. I hate to miss her wedding. She will be such a beautiful bride, and J.J. will be a handsome groom."

Kelly only smiled and listened to Mrs. Phelps's frail heart. This was the hardest part of being a doctor. There was very little she could do except to make her patient as comfortable as possible. Oh, how she wished the hospice program was in place already. She'd been working to get it going for a couple of years, and, if luck was with them, it would be up and running in a few months.

But too late for Mrs. Phelps.

AT SEVEN FORTY-FIVE on Friday morning Kelly heard a car drive up in front and a door slam. She lifted a slat on the miniblind to look out. Why she bothered, she didn't know. As always, it was Gladys Sowell, her maid, climbing from the back seat of Naconiche's only taxi and gathering her black coat around her. Taxi fare was part of her pay. There were no buses in Naconiche, but the taxi fare was nominal and the driver, Gladys's cousin, dependable.

A stocky woman with graying hair gathered up in a bun, Gladys was in her midfifties but looked older. She arrived every Monday, Wednesday, and Friday at seven forty-five on the button to feed the cats and Kelly, do laundry and keep the house spotless. A better housekeeper than she was a cook, she also cleaned the office rooms every afternoon at a reduced rate in exchange for medical attention. Since she was a terrible hypochondriac, Gladys probably got the best end of the deal, but she was a legacy along with the retiring doctor's practice.

Kelly finished dressing and walked into the kitchen where Gladys was feeding the cats and talking baby talk to them. Rocky and Pierre adored Gladys, and they were winding themselves around her legs as she pulled off her coat and put on her apron. Kelly had given her the coat last Christmas.

"Mornin', Dr. Kelly. How 'bout some bacon and eggs and biscuits?"

"Just fruit and cereal this morning, thanks." Gladys's idea of breakfast was greasier than anything at the City Grill. "How are you today?"

"Only tolerable. I had a sour stomach all night last night, and it kept me up and down a right smart."

"Have you been taking your medicine and watching your diet?"

"I've run out of them little purple capsules."

Kelly knew it was futile to scold Gladys about her diet. "I'll leave some samples at the office for you."

"And I'm out of my nerve pills, too."

"I'll get some from my bag." She kept a supply of Gladys's harmless "nerve pills" in an unmarked vial and dispensed them a few at a time.

"I'll have you some oatmeal done in just a jiffy. It's cold as a cast-iron commode out there, and you need something to stick to your ribs. You're likely to be busy today."

Gladys turned out to be right. Kelly had a booger of a day. It seemed that half her patients had ailments, and two emergencies kept her at the hospital until after eleven that night. Even her cats, Pierre and Rocky, yowled at her when she walked in the door.

"Sorry, guys," she said as she scooped some food into their dishes and gave them fresh water. "I'm pooped. Don't wake me early in the morning or you're toast."

She fell into bed and slept until almost eight. She would have slept longer except that she had two phone calls. One was a patient in labor, the other was Nonie Outlaw. She returned Miss Nonie's call on her way to the hospital.

"Dr. Kelly, I'm at my wit's end," Miss Nonie said. She sounded distraught and near tears. "It's Cole."

Kelly's heart gave a lurch. "What's wrong?"

"He refuses to go to J.J. and Mary Beth's wedding. We couldn't even pry him out to go to the rehearsal and dinner last night. Everybody in the family has tried to talk to him, but he's a stubborn as Vick Trawick's mule. I—I thought that since you seem to have a way with Cole that perhaps you could persuade him."

"Does he have a suit to wear?"

"Frank was going to lend him one, but nobody would care if he came in pajamas and bathrobe."

He would, Kelly thought. "I'm on my way to the hospital now, Miss Nonie, but tell Frank that I'll drop by and pick up the dress clothes when I'm done. The wedding's at three, isn't it?"

"Yes, but the clothes are already at the inn. Everything is hanging in a bag in the office. Frank left it there last night—in case Cole changed his mind."

"I'll do my best, Miss Nonie. Stop worrying about Cole and enjoy the day."

BY THE TIME Kelly got home, showered, tamed her hair and dressed in a rust-colored outfit, it was after one-thirty. She ate half a protein bar on the way to the Twilight Inn.

When she walked into the office, she saw the garment bag hanging on a hook behind the desk. Picking up the clothes, she took a deep breath then knocked on the door to the apartment.

Cole opened the door wearing a white T-shirt and a pair of the new sweatpants she'd bought. He gave her the once-over, then smiled. "You look mighty fine, Red. Going somewhere?"

"I am. To a wedding, and I need a date."

"Can't help you there. But I can offer you a cup of coffee."

"Got any brownies left?" she asked as she breezed by him with the garment bag.

"Nope. Ate the last one this morning for breakfast."

"With your eggs?"

"Instead of my eggs."

"Works for me," Kelly said. "Had lunch?"

"Yep. You?"

"Yep. Take off your pants."

He looked amused. "I think we've had this conversation before."

"A slight variation." She unzipped the bag and took out the dark suit pants. "Put these on instead."

"I'm not going to the wedding, Red."

"Don't call me Red. And you already told me that you're not going to the wedding with me. You did, however, ask me out for coffee, and how would it look with you in sweats and me in my finery?"

"In," he said.

"In?"

"I asked you *in* for coffee, not out."

She waved her hand in dismissal. "I prefer out. Need help with your pants?"

"Yeah."

It was a dare if she'd ever heard one.

"Okeydokey." She stuck her thumbs in the elastic waistband of his sweatpants and peeled them down. Thankfully he was wearing underwear. "Lift your right foot. Now your left. Good."

She kicked off her shoes and got into an awkward semisquat behind him to help him put on the dress slacks. The process was a struggle, but they finally made it. The legs were just a tad too short, but she didn't mention it. She figured that with him sitting in his wheelchair nobody would notice. The white shirt was snug but fit well enough.

By the time they had buttoned all the buttons, a fine line of sweat beaded his upper lip. Kelly said, "Let's sit down and rest a while. Want some juice? Orange, tomato, apple?"

"Orange would be good."

She poured juice while he eased into his recliner.

He emptied the glass when she handed it to him, then he leaned back and closed his eyes.

After a few minutes, she touched his arm. "Ready to put on the tie?"

He opened one eye and frowned. "Red, I'm not sure I can manage a tie."

"I can."

"You're a woman of many talents."

"You'd better believe it. I mastered the art when my dad broke his arm."

"When was that?"

"A while back, but I figure it's like riding a bicycle," she said. "It will come back to me. Sit up a little." She slipped the blue silk tie under his collar and expertly knotted it. "There you go."

"I'm impressed."

"As well you should be." She glanced down at his gray cotton socks and rose to retrieve shoes and dress socks from the bag.

Frank had thoughtfully provided black dress loafers that would slip on easily. Problem was, they didn't slip on easily.

"Push," she said as she knelt on the floor at his feet. "Harder."

"Darlin', I can push from now till kingdom come, and my foot isn't going in that shoe. Let me see it." When he looked inside the loafer, Cole said, "No wonder. It's too short and too narrow. I wear a thirteen double E."

"Good Lord, and I thought my foot was big." Kelly glanced at her watch. It was almost two-thirty. "Don't you have some other shoes?"

"Under the bed." He nodded toward the other room.

Kelly went looking, but all she found were the furry moccasins. She came back holding one in each hand. "These?"

"Yep."

Restraining herself from rolling her eyes, she said, "Let me make a quick call."

She phoned Olsen's, the only men's store in town

that sold something other than Western wear and work clothes. They didn't have any dress shoes in Cole's size; they'd sold the last pair to Stanley Bickham last Thursday. They had one pair of brown sandals left over from summer. She even called the store that carried cowboy boots, hoping to find something nice in his size. The only things they had to fit were two pair of rubber boots and some tan steel-toed loggers.

Knowing that there wasn't time to drive to Travis Lake and back, Kelly grabbed the fur-lined moccasins. "At least these will keep your toes warm," she said as she slipped them on his feet. "Stand up and let's put on the coat."

The fit wasn't too bad. "You look very handsome," she told him.

"For a sausage?"

"Maybe the coat's a little tight across the shoulders, but if you don't button it, it's fine. Let me get your wheelchair."

"I'll use the walker."

"We'll use the chair. Listen to the doctor."

"Darlin', you're not my doctor."

They finally compromised and took both.

While Cole buckled his seat belt, Kelly anxiously checked her watch and prayed that her timing would be right.

She drove to a convenience store, hurried in to make her purchase and came out with two small foam cups. She handed one to Cole.

"What's this?" he asked.

"Coffee. I told you we were going out for coffee."

He took a sip and frowned. ''It tastes like engine sludge.''

She tried it. The stuff was ghastly. She dumped both cups in the trash and drove to the church. He didn't even comment as she parked in the side lot.

''I thought that since we were dressed up and out anyway, we might go to the wedding,'' she said.

That amused expression of his was back again. ''You did, huh?''

''You'll go?''

''Red, for most of my adult life I've been around the worst kind of scum who can lie easier than they can tell the truth. Not much gets by me, and you didn't even come close.''

''If you knew my intentions, why did you go along so easily?''

''I'm a pushover for redheads.'' He winked.

''You really wanted to come, didn't you?''

He shrugged and glanced away.

It was that pride again, Kelly thought. He could have never gotten dressed by himself, and he didn't want to ask for help or be a burden to any of his family. Lord, the male ego was unbelievable.

Once he got into his wheelchair, she pushed him into the church and to the side door of the sanctuary. J.J. stood there with the minister and his brothers Frank and Sam.

J.J. broke into a big grin and slapped Cole on the back. '''Bout damn time you got here. We're fixin' to start.''

''Let's take our places, gentlemen,'' the minister said, opening the door.

He went in and J.J. and Frank followed. Sam, the

youngest brother and a Texas Ranger, grabbed the handles of the chair and started wheeling Cole in behind the others.

"Hold it, Sam!" Cole whispered. "I'm not going with y'all. Hell, I've got on Daddy's house shoes."

"Shut up, Cole," Sam said. "And smile."

Chapter Four

"You may kiss your bride," the minister said, and
J.J. planted a good one on her.

When the new couple was introduced to the con-
gregation, the entire assembly rose and burst into
thunderous applause. There was a packed house.
Since this was Mary Beth's second marriage, she and
J.J. had originally planned an intimate wedding with
only family and a few friends, but because most of
the town felt a party to their courtship, they didn't
want to leave out anyone and risk hurt feelings. They
had solved the problem by posting a notice in the
newspaper.

Kelly had slipped into a vacant seat at the end of
the front pew, planning to wheel Cole out the side
door when the ceremony was over. She grinned when
her plans went awry. Dixie, one of the bridesmaids,
grabbed Cole's chair and pushed him down the aisle
behind the bride and groom and the other two pairs
of attendants.

While the guests left for the reception at the VFW
hall—the only place in town big enough to handle the
crowd—the wedding party assembled back in the

church for picture taking. Cole wanted no part of it, but his family insisted that he stay. He endured about fifteen minutes of posing, then signaled for Kelly.

"Tired?" she asked as she wheeled him outside.

"Not particularly. I'm just not much on saying cheese for a camera."

"Your being there meant a lot to your family."

He nodded.

As soon as they were in her car, she pulled out of the parking lot and turned left. After a block or two, Cole said, "Isn't the motel in the other direction?"

She nodded.

"Where are you headed?"

"To the reception. I'm hungry. I want one of Buck's shrimp puffs and a piece of wedding cake."

"Who is Buck?" Cole asked.

"You haven't met him yet? He's Mary Beth's assistant at the tearoom. He and her staff are in charge of catering."

"Why don't you drop me off at the inn, and then you can go on and enjoy yourself."

"Mmm," Kelly said as if she were actually considering it. "No, I don't think so. I'd rather have a date."

"A date? This is more like a kidnapping than a date. And I imagine that you could do better than me."

"Not really. The pickings are pretty slim around Naconiche."

"I can't believe that men aren't lined up outside your door."

She laughed. "They are. But they usually have sinus infections or prostate problems."

SOMEBODY HAD REALLY fixed up the place, Cole thought as he looked around the old hall. Blue tablecloths and Christmas arrangements decorated the vintage bingo tables, and potted trees and shrubs strung with lights lined the walls. A small band was setting up in the corner.

"Looks nice," Cole said as he pushed his walker beside Kelly.

"Yes. Florence did a good job."

"Florence?"

"Florence Russo, Dixie's mother-in-law. She's a retired decorator who moved here from Dallas. She helps out part-time at the Twilight Inn."

"I can't believe that little Dixie Anderson is grown and married," Cole said.

"And has six kids."

"God, I'm getting old. Last time I remember her, she and Ellen and Mary Beth were high school cheerleaders."

"You haven't spent much time in Naconiche, have you?"

"Only a holiday here and there. And those were quick trips in and out to see the family. I joined the Houston Police Department the week after I graduated from college."

As they moved toward a table, Cole was waylaid by a mob of people, several of them buddies from school days. Most of them had beer bellies and a few were bald or getting that way fast. They looked like their daddies. Everybody seemed glad to see him, and nobody paid much attention to his moccasins. Except Bull Bickham. He and Bull had played football together when he was in high school.

"Wish I could trade shoes with you," Bull said. "These new ones I got on are hell on my bunion. I would've taken them back to the store 'cept my wife wouldn't let me wear my brogans."

Gradually he and Kelly made their way to one of the reserved tables. Flagging, he was more than ready to sit down when he got there. He'd insisted on using his walker instead of the wheelchair, and bedamned if he'd admit that Kelly was right when she'd argued against it.

"How about something cold to drink?" Kelly asked.

"I wouldn't mind some of that," he said, nodding toward the champagne fountain.

"Sorry. You'll have to drink with the teetotalers. Be right back."

He watched her go, enjoying the swing of her hips as she walked away.

"Leave it to you to grab the best-looking woman in town."

Cole glanced up and grinned at his youngest brother, Sam, the only one in the family taller than he was. "You got it. So hands off. How did you sneak away?"

"I didn't sneak. The rest of the family will be along in a minute. You okay?"

"Fine. How's rangering these days?"

Sam Bass Outlaw was a member of the elite Texas Rangers. He'd wanted to be one since he was a kid, and after a determined rise through the highway patrol, he'd made the cut two years before and was chosen to fill the only opening the Rangers had vacant in a while.

"Can't complain," Sam said.

"I've never known you to do anything else," a tall, leggy brunette said as she strode up to them.

"Hey, Ding-a-ling," Cole said, falling into his pet name for his sister.

"Hey, Big Buzzer," Belle said as she leaned down to peck him on the cheek. "You doing okay?"

"Fine. Have I told you that you're looking gorgeous today—for an FBI agent?"

She grinned. "Thanks. I like your shoes."

Cole laughed. As the baby sister of four rambunctious brothers, she'd learned early on how to give as good as she got. Belle would tangle with a wildcat—and win.

Kelly returned with her hands full and managing to juggle an extra plate on her arm.

"Let me get that for you," Sam said, relieving her of the refreshments she carried.

"Thanks. You must be Sam."

"I am," Sam said with a smooth smile. "And you're…?"

"With me," Cole said. He introduced Kelly to his brother and sister, and then the rest of the family arrived, including the bride and groom, and the party went into full swing.

Some time later, Cole watched as Sam led Kelly around the dance floor. He felt a twinge of envy. Hell, he felt more than a twinge when he saw his brother's arm around her waist. Cole wanted to rip off that arm and beat him with it. Crazy feeling.

"I like your doctor," Belle said.

"She's not my doctor."

"Coulda fooled me. You're looking at her like you could eat her with a spoon."

"I mean she's not my *doctor*. She's not treating me. Kelly's just a...friend."

"Uh-huh," Belle said, as if she didn't believe a word of it.

"We only met a few days ago." Had it only been a few days? Seemed longer. But then the days stretched interminably since he'd been shot. "How do you like Colorado?"

"I love it. I'm looking forward to some skiing soon. You'll have to come visit."

"I don't imagine that I'd be too swift on skis."

"You're not going to be out of commission forever," Belle said. "It will take a while, but you'll heal. When are you planning to go back to work?"

He shrugged. "I have no plans. How long are you going to be in town?"

"Not long. I could only get away for a weekend. Wish I could stay longer, but I'm flying out of Dallas tomorrow evening."

"Now that you're in a field office, are you enjoying your work?"

Belle hesitated for a moment, then said, "Sure."

Cole cocked an eyebrow at her. He knew his little sister like a book. From the time she could toddle, she'd always come to him with her problems. And he'd been able to help her with most of them—everything from thumping Sam for burying her Barbie to wiping her tears over missing a word on a spelling test. "What's wrong?"

She sighed. "Cole, have you wondered if you became a cop because law enforcement was a family tradition or if it was really what you wanted?''

"Nope. It's always been what I wanted. I think that Kojac and Dirty Harry may have pushed me toward homicide, but I always wanted to be a cop. Are you having second thoughts, Ding?''

"Oh, I don't know. Maybe sometimes. But I've worked so long and so hard to get where I am, I'm not ready to chuck it all yet.'' She smiled, leaned over and kissed his cheek. "I'm so happy to see you doing well, Big Buzzer. The last time I saw you, I was worried. You looked pretty awful.''

"The last time you saw me, I was in ICU.''

"With about a hundred tubes coming out of you or going in. Pale is not your best color. I donated blood for you.''

"Is *that* why I've been growing boobs?''

Belle laughed and swatted his arm. "I wish you could come dance with me.''

"I do, too, darlin'. I do, too.''

KELLY HAD ALWAYS loved weddings and all the rituals involved, so she had a wonderful time, oohing when the newlyweds cut the cake and aahing when J.J. took Mary Beth onto the floor for their first dance. Kelly had done a fair amount of dancing herself— with every man in the Outlaw family, except Cole, and with several of her patients.

"Looks as if you found another eligible Outlaw,'' her friend Carrie said when they met at the champagne fountain.

"Sam's too young for me, so you must mean Cole," Kelly said. "I don't imagine a romance between us. He's like a bird with a broken wing right now, but when he's healed, he'll fly away.''

''Maybe not. It would be nice having you as a sister-in-law. Free medical care and all that.''

Kelly laughed. ''I think a good insurance policy would be a better bet. I don't see Cole as the marrying kind—and certainly not to someone like me.''

''What do you mean 'someone like' you?''

''As my former fiancé put it—someone who smells like a hospital and can't sit through an entire movie without an emergency. He said marrying me would be like committing bigamy, since I'm already married to my job.''

''What a turkey.''

''Luckily I realized that in time to cancel the wedding invitations. But I think he was right. Not many men can handle the demands of a doctor's life—except maybe another doctor.''

''Or a cop,'' Carrie said.

''I can't believe we're having this conversation,'' Kelly said. ''Trust me, there is absolutely no chance of a relationship between Cole and me. None. Zip. *Nada.*''

Carrie grinned. ''But you will have to admit he's a hunk.''

''Really? I hadn't noticed.''

''Li-ar,'' Carrie singsonged.

Kelly only smiled, and they parted company.

Oh, she'd noticed Cole Younger was a hunk. Every female hormone in her body was on red alert. She glanced toward him and found him watching her.

He winked.

Good Lord, could he read her mind?

She quickly turned back to the champagne fountain, grabbed a glass, and held it under a spigot. Her hand shook.

What was the matter with her? She chugalugged the wine and hurried to the ladies' room.

WHEN SHE CAME OUT of the ladies' room, Kelly saw that the party was still going strong, but Cole wasn't. He looked tired. She slipped out to her car and got his wheelchair.

Once back at the table she tapped him on the shoulder. "How about I waltz you out of here, big guy?"

"Are you going to insist on leading?" Cole asked.

"Naturally. And get a move on. My coach is about to turn into a pumpkin."

"Need any help?" Sam asked.

"Not a bit," Cole replied, standing and slipping into the chair.

"You can bring the walker," Kelly said.

"I'll take it," Belle said. "You go dance with Sally Easy again," she told her youngest brother.

"Easly. Sally Easly."

"Could have fooled me," Belle said. "She's been drooling all over you for an hour or more."

"Get off his case, Ding," Cole said. "Can the kid help it if he's irresistible?"

Belle looked Sam up and down. "Irresistible? Him? I don't get it." She hooked the folded walker over her arm and led the way around the edge of the crowd.

Kelly helped Cole into her car, then she and Belle stowed the chair and walker in the back.

"Is he going to be okay, Dr. Kelly?" Belle asked quietly.

"Cole? He's going to be fine. It's just going to take some time and a lot of work."

Before they left, Belle stuck her head in the window and gave Cole a peck on the cheek. "I want to spend some time with you before I leave, Big Buzzer."

"Come by for breakfast in the morning," he told her. "I'll make the coffee. You bring the breakfast."

"You're on."

As they drove away, Cole ripped off his tie, unbuttoned his shirt collar and leaned back against the headrest. "Thanks for rescuing me. I was ready to get out of there. I feel like I've been chewed up, spit out and stepped on."

"I noticed you were looking a little tired. And my feet are killing me. I haven't danced so much in years."

"Are you bragging or complaining?"

"My feet are complaining. I don't spend much time in high heels."

"Me, either."

Kelly chuckled. "I doubt if you could find any in your size. Aren't you glad now that you went to the wedding and the reception?"

Cole smiled. "Yeah. Yeah, I am. But I'm worn out."

They arrived at the Twilight Inn a few moments later, and she wheeled him inside to his apartment.

When he stood to move to his recliner, Kelly helped him off with his coat. She started to unbutton his shirt, and when Cole put his hands on her hips to steady himself, something strange happened to her breathing. A woozy feeling washed over her, her heartbeat accelerated and her fingers fumbled the buttons. She caught herself, palms against his chest. "Sorry, I must visited that fountain once too often."

"How much champagne did you have?"

"Only a couple of glasses." Kelly knew it wasn't the wine causing her reactions; it was the intimate contact. She was doing fine until he touched her.

Cole's fingers tightened on her hips, and she glanced up. He didn't say anything. He didn't have to. His eyes were almost black, and she could feel the pounding of his heart against her fingers.

Trying to ignore the sexual awareness that steamed like an overheated radiator, she quickly disposed of the shirt and unbuckled his belt. When she reached for his fly zipper, his hand covered hers. "I'll do that later."

"Don't be silly. You're exhausted, and I don't mind helping."

"Darlin', I may too tuckered to pucker, but some parts of me don't seem to have gotten the message."

Automatically she glanced down and didn't know whether to laugh or blush. "Well, at least you know everything is in working order."

"Yeah, there's that. But the timing is lousy."

"I could come back later." Had she really said that? She couldn't believe she'd said that. What had gotten into her?

She didn't have time to bemoan her gaffe any longer because Cole seemed to have gotten a second wind. His arms went around her, and he pulled her into a kiss that blew her away, stole her breath and set her reeling. His mouth was greedy, and her response was just as hungry. She plastered herself against him and savored every sensual moment.

Her pulse raced and her belly vibrated—

Kelly went still. Her belly vibrated again.

"Sorry," she said, pushing away. "My pager."

"Ignore it." He reached for her mouth.

"Can't. I'm not on call. It must be an emergency. I have to go. And you need to rest."

He cocked one dark eyebrow. "Darlin', right now rest is the last thing on my mind." He sighed and loosened his arms. "Call me later."

Chapter Five

Kelly charged in the back door of the hospital and collided with Warren Iverson. "Sorry," she said and tried to step around him.

He blocked her path. "Careful, Dr. Martin. You could have injured someone. Have you been drinking?"

She wanted to clobber him. He knew very well she'd toasted the bride and groom—and had a second glass of champagne. He'd been at the reception taking notes.

"Excuse me, I have an emergency." She pushed past him and hurried for the nurses' station. Let the old goat stand there and sputter. She didn't care.

The news on her elderly patient, Mrs. Phelps, was not good.

After Kelly checked her, she said to the nurse, "I think you should call her niece immediately." Mrs. Phelps's only relative was a niece in Shreveport. "And her pastor."

Kelly elevated the frail woman's bed to make breathing easier, smoothed damp gray tendrils back from her forehead with a cool cloth and sat holding her hand until someone from the church came to stay with her. Dammit, this was a perfect example of the town's need for hospice care. She felt totally inadequate. Nothing in medical school had really prepared her for having to say goodbye to her patients. Oh, there was the usual admonition about staying objective and emotionally detached, but she'd never been able to do it. She cared too much.

But could anyone care *too* much?

She said a silent prayer and slipped quietly from the room.

When Kelly got home, she took a long bath and put on soft knit lounging pants and a top. She heated a can of chicken noodle soup, but she ate only a bite or two.

Restless, she turned on the TV, then turned it off.

Neither Rocky nor Pierre seemed in the mood to cuddle. They had retreated to their hidey-holes.

Pacing didn't help. She wanted to scream or weep or…something. But she didn't dare start crying or she might not stop. She hugged herself and shivered. She desperately needed—

"To hell with this!"

She grabbed her keys and hurried to her car. The car headed toward the Twilight Inn on autopilot.

When she arrived, Kelly hesitated before she knocked on the apartment door. He probably wasn't even there. With all his family in town, he was probably visiting with them or—

The door opened.

Cole smiled when he saw her. "I thought I heard someone drive up. I'm glad it was you. Come in."

She strode past him and stood stiffly in the middle of the room. Only a table lamp by his recliner was on, and a paperback book lay opened and facedown on the chair seat. She nervously smoothed her wild hair. "I look like a witch."

"You look like an angel. Maybe a little wild-eyed. What's wrong?"

She took a deep breath. "I need— I need—"

"What do you need?" he asked softly.

"I need to be held."

He opened his arms wide, and she flew into them.

Being enclosed in his warmth and strength felt heavenly, and her head fit perfectly against his shoulder. Tension eased as she melted against his chest. Even the walker rails between them didn't bother her...at first.

Then she gradually realized what those rails meant. "I'm sorry," she said, pushing away. "You don't need to be holding me up."

"Sure I do."

"No. You don't."

"Then let's move to the couch, and I can do a better job of it."

Kelly didn't argue. She was too forlorn to argue. Mindful of his injuries, she cuddled against him on the couch, and he held her. More tension eased, and she allowed herself to free-fall into the comfort and security he provided. He held her for the longest time and didn't say a word. And the longer he held her, and the more she savored the solace of his arms, the more she realized how desperately she had needed this for years—someone to lean on now and then.

She was a strong woman. She'd had to be to make it as a doctor, but even the strongest person needed TLC once in a while.

"Want to talk about it?" Cole asked quietly.

Kelly shook her head. "Not now." She burrowed closer. "This feels so good."

"Glad to oblige." He rubbed his chin against the top of her head. "Your hair is so soft. I thought it would feel different." He sifted strands through his fingers.

"It's like kinky kitten fur," she mumbled against his chest.

He chuckled and she felt the rumble against her cheek. "It's like a blazing fire. I love your hair."

"You should try to brush it in the mornings."

"Be glad to give it a try." He nuzzled her forehead.

The nuzzling became kisses, and slowly the kisses became caresses. She hadn't worn a bra, and soon she wasn't wearing a top. She ought to stop this, she thought, but his touch consoled such a deep ache that it mesmerized her, and she just couldn't stop.

When he stroked her breasts and drew them into his mouth, she lost it, and all thought of stopping ended. She gave herself over to glorious sensation.

Piece by piece their clothes landed in heaps on the floor as they fondled and kissed and explored. He whispered praises for her body, and she basked in the praise; he kissed her deeply, groaned his desire, and she soared.

"I want you," he said.

"I want you, too."

"I'm not sure I can. My hip, my—"

Her lips stopped the words. "Let the doctor handle it. Lie back."

She knelt, straddling his hips, and leaned over to kiss him as she slowly slipped herself onto him.

"Oh, darlin'," he groaned. "Take it easy."

"Am I hurting you?"

"Not hardly. But I want this to last." He drew her down to take a nipple into his mouth and suck hard.

It sent her through the roof.

"Forget lasting," she said as she moved up and down in a frantic pace.

They both climaxed powerfully and quickly. Backs bowed, release shuddered their bodies and drew gasps and groans.

Still kneeling with him inside, she snuggled against him, her head on his shoulder. He hugged her tightly, and she savored the last throbs of their passion.

"If this kills me," he said, "just tell everybody that I died happy."

Kelly laughed. "I don't think you're in danger of dying."

"Then just throw a blanket over me and wake me in the morning."

"Cold?"

"No, but I might be when the lather wears off. We don't have any clothes on."

"Sure we do," she said, rubbing her foot along his leg. "We have our socks on."

He chuckled and kissed her forehead. "You are some kind of woman."

"What kind is that?"

"The good kind. I've had a hard-on for you since the first time I saw you."

"Really?"

"Yep. You've been on my mind a lot."

Smiling smugly, she twirled damp strands of chest hair around her finger. She'd never thought of herself as the object of anyone's sexual fantasies.

Reluctant to move she stayed there until the chill

became uncomfortable. Finally she rose, snagged her clothes and went to the bathroom.

She'd barely had time to dress when Cole tapped on the door. He'd pulled on sweatpants.

"Your cell phone is ringing."

Kelly knew what the message would be before she answered, and she was right. "I have to go," she told Cole.

"Emergency?"

"Not exactly. One of my patients just died."

"I'm sorry." He pulled her into his arms.

"Me, too. She was a sweet old lady, but there was nothing I could do except let her go."

"That must hurt." He kissed her forehead.

Kelly nodded. "Being here with you helped, but I—I feel awkward about it now. I want you to know that I don't ordinarily hop into bed with men I barely know. In fact, I can't remember the last time I hopped into bed with anybody."

He smiled. "Glad I was handy when you decided to hop. I was afraid that I was a mercy case."

"Not hardly." This time she smiled. "Thanks."

"I don't think thanks are necessary under the circumstances. I wish you didn't have to go."

"It's a doctor's life." She allowed herself only a brief kiss, then left.

COLE PUSHED BACK in his recliner and closed his eyes. He felt on top of the world and totally wrung out at the same time. Dr. Kelly Martin was one hell of a woman—everything he'd fantasied and more. If he'd met her before he'd been hurt, he would have gone after her with a vengeance. But now...

Hell, he couldn't even button his shirt without

breaking into a sweat. Or make love to her the way he wanted. Even if he hadn't been lousy at relationships, she was way beyond his reach. A woman like her didn't need to be saddled with a cripple.

Earlier she'd been hurting, and he'd been handy. He wasn't about to complain, but he wasn't going to make anything more of it, either. Damn, she'd felt good. Too good.

It suddenly struck him that they hadn't used any protection. He hadn't even thought about it at the time. He slapped his head. What had he been thinking?

That was the problem. He hadn't been thinking. And he certainly didn't have any condoms in his duffel bag. Needing any hadn't even crossed his mind. Holy cripes!

But Kelly was a doctor. She knew how to protect herself from pregnancy. She was probably on the pill or something. And he didn't have any dread diseases. God knows he'd been checked enough. He'd have to ask her about protection if there was ever a repeat performance.

Not that he figured there would be one. If he had her pegged right—and he was an excellent judge of character—tomorrow she'd be sorry about what had happened between them, embarrassed and apologetic.

And that would be the end of it.

THEY HADN'T USED any protection!

It didn't dawn on Kelly until she was lying in bed that night. She jackknifed up. Holy cow! What an idiot she was. Where were her brains?

Just relax, she told herself. It was unlikely that she would get pregnant from a single encounter—especially since she had some problems that would make conceiving extremely difficult for her in any case.

Still she thought back to her last menses and counted days on her fingers. No, not a fertile period. She breathed easier and dropped down to her pillow.

Tomorrow she'd raid the sample closet and put a few condoms in her purse. Next time, she'd be prepared.

Next time?

Would there be a next time?

Darned right. Cole Outlaw was a virile, desirable man, and she was enormously attracted to him. Why shouldn't she enjoy herself with him? She wasn't looking for happily ever after; neither was he. He'd soon be healed and gone back to Houston.

A tiny part of her fleetingly imagined them standing together at the altar where J.J. and Mary Beth had stood that afternoon, but she quickly dismissed it. Kelly doubted that she would ever marry. And Cole didn't strike her as the kind to settle down in Naconiche with a wife and picket fence.

Rocky jumped onto her bed and rubbed her with his head. She stroked his fur, and he snuggled beside her. Pierre soon joined them.

"Where were you guys when I needed you?"

Rocky purred, but Pierre only yawned.

"WHAT IS *THIS*?" Cole asked his sister after she'd spooned a mound of glop into his bowl.

"Oatmeal with flaxseed and raisins," Belle said. "It's good. I eat it every morning."

"When I suggested that you bring breakfast, I was hoping for something along the lines of sausage and eggs and Mama's biscuits."

"Too much cholesterol. That stuff will kill you. And I brought some soy milk."

"*Soy* milk? Sounds disgusting."

"It's quite tasty," Belle said, "and very good for you." She poured a couple of glugs over the oatmeal.

He stared at the mess in his bowl. Was this a joke or was she serious?

"Eat up, Big Buzzer." Belle took a bite from her bowl.

She was serious.

He took a bite from his. It was warm and slightly lumpy with a kind of nutty taste. "Not too bad."

"Told you."

He dumped a couple of spoonfuls of sugar in it before Belle could stop him and managed to get it all down. He wouldn't hurt his little sister's feelings for the world.

They finished their breakfast, such as it was, and settled back with a cup of coffee. Rather Cole had coffee; Belle drank some sort of herbal concoction that reminded him of grass clippings. He could tell there was something she wanted to say, but they talked around it for a while.

Finally Cole said, "Honey, what's on your mind?"

She stared into her cup for several moments, then ran her finger around its rim as if weighing her thoughts. "I'm seriously considering resigning from the FBI."

"To do what?"

She didn't look up. "To raise horses, to write, to paint. To get married."

"Who's the guy with the horses?"

She smiled. "Not much gets by you, does it? His name is Matt Carson."

"Any relation to Kit?"

Belle grinned. "Distant cousins, I think."

"I thought you loved being an agent."

"The love affair has cooled. I've begun to hate my job. The politics are driving me crazy. On the other hand, I love living on the ranch—"

Cole frowned, then said gruffly, "You've already moved in with this yahoo?"

"Don't get your shorts in a wad, Big Buzzer. I'm not a kid anymore."

"Sorry."

"I've been living on his ranch for about three months. It's beautiful, and I love it there. And I love Matt. But he's not the reason I want to leave the FBI. I've been thinking about it for a long time."

"Then go for it, darlin'. Life's too short not to do what makes you happy."

"And what about you?" Belle said. "Does being a cop really make you happy?"

Cole thought for a minute. "I'm not sure that I'd say happy, but it's what I know and enjoy. I'm a damned good cop. *Was* a damned good cop. And if I could go back to my job tomorrow, I'd be out of here like a shot."

"Don't you think you'll be able to return to work?"

He shrugged. "The doctor and the therapists seem to think I can, but I don't know. It's going to be a long haul, and I'm not willing to ride a desk until I retire. We'll just have to wait and see."

Belle squeezed his hand. "You're going to be fine. I can feel it in my bones."

"Have you told Mom and Dad about your new plans?"

"I haven't talked to anybody in the family yet. I wanted to fly it by you first."

"I say, if you're really sure about what you want, then go for it. Everybody else will say the same thing."

Belle hugged him. "You always make me feel better." She poured him another cup of coffee. "Now tell me about this lovely redhead you're keeping company with."

"Nothing to tell."

She cocked one eyebrow. "You wouldn't want to be hooked up to a lie detector and repeat that, would you?"

He only laughed and changed the subject.

Belle had barely left when Sam showed up.

His youngest brother handed him a foil-wrapped package. "Mama sent you some sausage and biscuits in case you couldn't eat that stuff that Belle brought. What's she into these days?"

"Health food. It wasn't too bad."

"Then I'll eat the biscuits and sausage."

"The hell you will," Cole said, grabbing the package.

Chapter Six

Kelly, with two warm pecan pies stowed in the back seat, drove to Frank Outlaw's big house outside of town. She hadn't wanted to accept the invitation to Sunday dinner—which was the noon meal in Naconiche—but Carrie had insisted.

"You have to come," Carrie had pled early Sunday morning. "I'm supposed to be hostess to the whole family, and I'm not even sure which fork goes where. What kind of daughter-in-law will Nonie and Wes think they're getting?"

"One that their son loves," Kelly had said. "And I'm sure that your mother wouldn't have allowed you past puberty without instilling all the social graces. Shall I pick up Cole?"

"No, I think Sam is doing that. Just come early and be my moral support."

Carrie Campbell was one tough lady; Kelly doubted that she needed support of any kind, but she agreed to come if she could bring something for the meal. So she had gone to early church, changed into casual clothes and baked pies.

When she arrived at Frank's house, Carrie wrapped

her in an embrace. "Oh, bless you, Kelly. I'm going out of my mind. What do I know about cooking? The housekeeper usually does that, and she's off today. She left instructions for the pot roast. Would you come see if it's done? Miss Nonie is bringing green beans and rolls, but I have to fix corn and mashed potatoes, and I don't know one end of a potato masher from the other. Frank and the kids have taken the cat and her kittens to the barn. Want a kitten? The little things are everywhere. They're really cute, but you can barely step without fear of squashing one."

Kelly laughed. "Thanks, but I don't want another kitten, and, yes, I'll check the pot roast. Calm down."

"I can't believe I'm dithering. I never *dither*. My *mother* dithered, for gosh sakes."

Knowing Carrie's bumpy history with her flighty and self-serving mother, Kelly understood how horrified her friend was by her behavior. "You're only a little anxious. Perfectly natural. Where's the kitchen?"

COLE POLISHED OFF his last bite of pie, then said, "Carrie, that was a great meal."

"Don't thank me," Carrie said. "All I did was turn on the oven and put the roast in. Kelly and your mother did the rest."

"Dr. Kelly, darlin'," Sam said, "you can cook, too? Will you marry me?"

"Oh, hush, Romeo," Belle said, "and grab your plate. You and I are going to clean up. And don't poke around. I want to go riding before I have to leave."

"You'll have to excuse my little sister," Sam said

to Kelly. "She's always been bossy." Nevertheless, he winked and started stacking dishes.

"Don't take my plate," Wes said. "I want another sliver of that pecan pie."

"Wes, you don't need any more pie," Nonie said. "You've already had to take the ice pick to your belt."

Wes patted his belly. "Darlin', you know I don't weigh an ounce more than I did ten years ago."

"That's true, Papa Bear," Belle said, kissing her father's cheek as she grabbed his plate, "but the sand has shifted."

Wes playfully popped at Belle's bottom with his napkin, but she danced away laughing.

Frank got up to pour another round of coffee. Katy, who was staying with Frank's family, and the twins helped Belle and Sam clear the table, then ran out to play.

Kelly had thoroughly enjoyed the meal, and Cole had seemed to, as well. The family appeared very at home here, which was only natural since they'd lived in the house for years and eaten many meals around the big dining-room table.

"Do you ever miss the old place, Mom?" Cole asked.

"Rarely," Miss Nonie said. "I'm only attached to the memories, not taking care of it. Your dad and I enjoy the apartment in town and being in the midst of things."

"You got that right," Wes said, rising. "I can sleep past sunup and don't have to worry about feeding livestock in the rain. I'm going to go see what the kids are into."

Soon everyone scattered in various directions, and only Kelly and Cole were left lingering over a cup of coffee.

"Sure you don't want to go riding with the others?" Cole asked her.

Kelly shook her head. "I haven't been on a horse in years."

"Belle and Sam are probably in the next county by now. Put either one of them on a horse, and they take off like greased lightning."

"Carrie will hold her own with them. She used to be a barrel racer."

"Carrie?" he said, looking surprised. "I figured her for a city girl."

"She is—sort of. But she spent her teens on a ranch."

"Have you been friends long?"

"We were sorority sisters in college, but I hadn't seen her in years until she showed up in Naconiche a few months ago."

"To work on the oil leases?" he said.

"Yes. We got reacquainted just in time to scandalize the town."

"Scandalize the town? That sounds interesting."

Kelly laughed. "Your mother talked Carrie and me into being in the Fall Follies, you know, the big town production for charity. Carrie and I sang and danced to 'Diamonds Are a Girl's Best Friend.'"

"What's so scandalous about that?"

"You should have seen our costumes—or what there was of them," she said. "Actually, most people got a kick out of our act, but the chairman of the hospital board almost had a coronary. He would have branded me with a scarlet letter if he could have. As it was, he raised a terrible stink.''

"Who's the chairman these days?"

"Warren Iverson."

"Warren Iverson?" Cole said. "How on earth did that prissy little prick get put in charge?"

She couldn't help chuckling at his characterization of her nemesis. "His father-in-law died, and Mr. Iverson took over the Trimble Candy Company. They employ a good number of people around here, and he's spread a lot of money around for various causes. He's on the board of several benevolent organizations."

"Warren Iverson," Cole said, shaking his head. "Who'd have ever thought he would amount to anything? I wonder how he talked Beulah Lee Trimble into marrying him?"

"That was before my time. I'm sure your mom knows."

"Do you still have it?" Cole asked.

"What?"

Cole grinned. "The costume. I'd like to see what I missed."

Kelly only laughed. Then she glanced at her watch. "I'm going to have to leave. I need to drive over to Travis Lake and shop for a couple of Christmas gifts and a new pair of sneakers for me."

"Mind if I go along with you? I could use a pair myself."

THEY ENDED UP with more than just her gifts and the two pair of athletic shoes—his the easy on and off kind. Cole also bought a pair of loafers. And since the fancy little photograph albums Kelly bought seemed like pretty good presents, he bought one for everybody in his family except the kids. They even came already wrapped in red paper. Couldn't beat that.

Wearing his new athletic shoes, Cole held the sacks in his lap, and Kelly pushed his chair through the crowded aisles of the large department store filled with Christmas shoppers. The steady buzz and bustle almost drowned out the holiday music piped overhead, and about a dozen elves scurried about spritzing various perfumes and handing out little samples of the potent stuff. Cole thought the store smelled like a high-priced cathouse.

The place got on his nerves. Since he'd been a cop he'd never been much of one for holiday spirit. It only meant that the crime rate went up. And he'd usually worked on Christmas Day so that the guys with children could be with their families. He wanted nothing more than to get out of the mad rush surrounding them, but on the other hand, knowing that it would be a while before he could get any clothes from his apartment in Houston, he figured that this might be his best opportunity to pick up some other things for himself.

As they passed by the men's department on the way out of the store he asked, "Do you mind if I stop by here for a minute?"

"Not at all. What do you need?"

"Something besides sweats and pajamas."

Maneuvering through the jam-packed displays was a bitch, but they located a stack of khakis, and he found a couple of pairs in his size. There were some shirts nearby, and, with Kelly's help, he picked out two of those along with a sweater and a jacket on sale. He wasn't nearly as concerned about choosing something that matched his eyes as she was. Blue was blue, brown was brown, gray was gray. All he wanted to do was grab something decent, pay and leave.

Kelly had other ideas.

"Aren't you going to try those on?" she asked.

"Naw. They're the size I always wear."

"But you've lost some weight. Those pants might not fit. And the sweater—well, sweaters don't all fit the same. You need to try them on."

It was hard to argue when Kelly had charge of the wheelchair. She pushed him toward the dressing room. A kid wearing dreadlocks and earrings with his snappy suit stopped them at the door. His gold badge identified him as Malcolm.

"'Scuse me, ma'am, but you can't go in there. That's the men's dressing room."

"I'm a doctor," Kelly said.

"Ma'am, I don't care if you're Queen Latifah, you can't go in there."

"But he needs help—"

"I'm here to serve," Malcolm said, grabbing the chair and tooling through the curtains.

Problem was, the chair wouldn't go in the little cubicle.

"I can manage from here," Cole told him.

"You sure?"

"Yeah. Just put the clothes in the dressing room and these packages in the chair when I get up."

Malcolm helped him get situated, then left. And, while it was a strain, Cole did manage just fine.

Until he started to take off the khakis.

The damned zipper got stuck.

He pulled and cursed and yanked. It wouldn't go up; it wouldn't go down. He tugged and sweated and turned the air blue, but it wouldn't budge. And he was exhausted from trying.

Cole was about to yell for Malcolm when the door flew open. Kelly stood there.

"Are you okay?" she asked.

He'd sooner be beaten with a blackjack than admit the truth, but he didn't have any choice. "Zipper's stuck," he mumbled.

"Which one?"

"The damned fly." He kept yanking, but it didn't help.

"Here," she said, "let me do it."

Two of them in the small cubicle was a tight squeeze, but he leaned against the wall while she knelt in front of him to work on the caught fabric. God, he felt like such a wuss, as helpless as a damned baby. And he hated having her see him that way. His ego, what there was left of it, had been knocked flat and stomped on.

"This is *really* hard," Kelly said.

"Tell me about it," Cole said.

The door flew open again.

"Hey," Malcolm said, "what's going on in here?"

"My zipper's stuck," Cole said as Kelly kept working with his fly.

"Uh-huh," Malcolm said, rolling his eyes as if he didn't believe a word of it.

"It is," Cole said.

About that time there was the unmistakable sound of a zipper sliding smoothly on its tracks.

Malcolm rolled his eyes again.

Cole wanted to deck him.

"Ma'am, you gotta get out of here. Customers are gonna be complaining," Malcolm said. "This ain't no motel."

Kelly looked as if she wanted to argue, but when Cole ground his teeth and nodded to her, she left.

"Pants fit?" Malcolm asked, not even masking a knowing smirk.

"The pants fit fine," Cole said quietly. "I'll wear them. Ring up everything. And wipe that expression off your face, or you'll be picking up your teeth in a paper sack."

Malcolm looked as if he were going to smart off again, but something in Cole's eyes or his tone of voice must have stopped him.

"Yes, sir. Will that be cash or charge?"

KELLY DIDN'T SAY a word until they were in the car, then she burst into laughter. "That kid thought that—"

"I know what he thought," Cole ground out. "I'm sorry he embarrassed you."

"Embarrassed me? He didn't embarrass me. I think it's a hoot." She started laughing again.

"I would appreciate it if you wouldn't mention this to anyone. If any of my brothers got wind of it, they would carry me high."

"My lips," she said, making a motion across her mouth, "are zipped." Another snort of laughter escaped.

Cole started laughing as well. It felt good to laugh. He'd been wound tighter than Dick's hatband.

As they drove back to Naconiche, Kelly said, "I can't believe it. A man who shops without grumbling."

"It's not my favorite activity, but I needed some clothes. I don't know how you women do it. I'm worn out."

"*You women?* Was that a sexist remark I heard?"

"Sorry. Guess I stepped in it again. Most of what I remember about my ex is that she was happiest in the mall with a handful of plastic."

"What a thing to be remembered for."

"How could I forget? She skipped out owing a bundle. It took me a long time to pay off her credit card debt."

"Why didn't she pay her own debt?" Kelly asked.

"Because she had a better lawyer than I did. She ended up marrying the bastard."

Kelly was quiet for a moment, then said, "I see."

Cole started to let it drop at that. He didn't want to rehash old news. Thinking about his wasted years with Sharon grated on him, and he sure as hell didn't like to discuss his marriage with anyone. But something made him want to explain to Kelly.

"Sharon and I probably should have never gotten married, but she…well, we did, and I tried to make the best of it. She didn't like being married to a cop. Hated it in fact. We tried counseling, and that didn't work. We were both miserable. She shopped. I found other things to do to keep from going home. One day she packed her clothes and left."

"No kids?"

Cole shook his head. Sharon hadn't wanted children. Didn't want to ruin her figure or have any "rugrats'' cutting into her time. Funny, since that was the reason he'd married her. She'd told him she was pregnant. He never knew if the miscarriage she'd claimed to have had while he was out of town was real or fake.

When they arrived back at the Twilight Inn, Kelly helped him inside with all his new stuff. He took her into his arms and said, ''Thanks for your help today.''

She gave him a peck on the cheek. ''You're welcome. Need me to help take off your pants?''

He grinned. ''Only if you'll let me help take off yours.''

''Sounds like a good trade, but unfortunately I don't have time. I have to be at a meeting in about fifteen minutes.''

''Can't you cancel?''

She shook her head. ''I'm chairman of the hospice committee, and the meeting took a long time to set up. It's important that I be there. How about a rain check?''

''Anytime. You know where to find me.'' He kissed her, and she responded for a moment, then broke away.

''I really have to go.''

As he watched her leave, Cole wondered if she really had a meeting or if she was already regretting getting something started with him.

Chapter Seven

Kelly pulled up in front of the bungalow just as Woodrow Bickham, a burly fellow who owned a construction company, arrived, and Noah Ware, the handsome blond doctor who was her suite mate, came as she was unlocking the front door. Florence Russo and Amos Whitaker were the other two members of the hospice committee. Florence was the retired interior decorator who occasionally helped Mary Beth at the Twilight Tearoom; Reverend Whitaker was minister of one of the local churches and the current president of the area ministerial alliance.

Empty except for a long table and a few folding chairs, the place smelled musty in the way that old houses did, especially those closed up for a long time. At least it was warm inside, thanks to Mr. Bickham who'd come by earlier and turned on the heat. The house had belonged to Althea Markham, now eighty-three, who had recently gone into the local assisted living facility. Mrs. Markham, a widow since World War II, had been the principal of the elementary school for many years before she retired and had been active in the community until her arthritis began taking its toll. A patient of both Kelly and Noah, she had donated her house to the hospice fund.

"I don't need the money," Mrs. Markham had said to Kelly, "and I don't have any family left. I want you to use my house as you see fit."

Only a block from the hospital and from Noah and Kelly's office, it was a lovely little place, three bedrooms and a bath, with lots of windows and a fireplace in the living room. Mr. Bickham had gone over it with a fine-tooth comb and was to report on his findings at the meeting that evening.

Kelly was eager for the others to arrive so that he could present his findings. Getting a hospice started in Naconiche had been her passion for the past two years. As a tribute to her younger sister whose last days had been made more bearable by the hospice workers, she had made the anonymous donation that funded the drive for an organization in town.

Florence, a tall, attractive woman with beautifully cropped white hair, was the next to arrive, then Reverend Whitaker, a former track star now in his forties, hurried in apologizing for being late. "Brother Johnson's prayer ran overlong," he said with a wink.

"No problem," Kelly said. "I know everyone is eager to hear Mr. Bickham's report, so I'll turn the floor over to him."

"The news is good," he said.

Kelly breathed a sigh of relief. The house was structurally sound, the zoning wasn't a problem, and, with a few modifications, the place could be turned into headquarters for a hospice center. Their next step, besides raising more funds, was to hire a director and begin licensing procedures.

Kelly felt like shouting as she drove home from the meeting. Bless Mrs. Markham's heart! She wanted to pull over and dance a jig, but Woodrow Bickham was driving behind her, and he'd probably think she was nuts. Instead, when she got home, she scooped up Rocky and said, "The hospice project is a go. Isn't that great?"

He only yowled and wiggled until she put him down.

So much for sharing her good news.

Still, she was about to burst to tell someone, she thought as she fed the cats and scanned the kitchen for something to eat. She poured a glass of milk, then grabbing the peanut butter jar, a sleeve of crackers and an apple, she carried the tray full of goodies to her bedroom and put it on the nightstand. After she dressed for bed and slipped under the covers, she reached for the tray, but her hand went to the telephone instead. Her finger seemed to automatically dial the Twilight Inn.

"Hello." Cole's voice sounded low and sexy. Or was it sleepy?

"Did I wake you?" she asked.

"No. I was just thinking about you."

"Something good I hope."

"Something very good," he said. "I was remembering how sweet your lips tasted and how hot your body felt."

"Is this going to be an obscene call?"

He chuckled. "Maybe. Have you ever had phone sex?"

"No. It never appealed to me before. I suppose I'm not an auditory person."

Cole chuckled again. "I prefer the real thing my-self. What's going on? Is your meeting over?"

"Yes, and it went very well. I'm happy to an-nounce that Naconiche is going to have a hospice center very soon—or within a year, at least. We still have a lot of work to do and a lot of money to raise, but we're really on our way. Someone donated a house to the fund, and tonight the inspector pro-nounced it sound, and, with some modifications, a good place for the center to be located."

"That's great news, Kelly."

"Yes, it is. I'm very excited about it. Noah and I have been trying to put this together for a long time."

"Noah?"

"Dr. Ware."

There was a long silence. "Are the two of you...close?" Cole asked.

"Sure. Besides sharing offices, we're colleagues and good friends."

"Only friends?"

Did she detect a hint of jealousy? It was her turn to chuckle. "His wife wouldn't stand for anything else."

Was that a sigh she heard?

"He's married?" Cole asked.

"Yes, with two teenagers and a three-year-old. Be-sides he's not my type."

"Oh?"

"No," she said. "I prefer brunettes."

"Oh," he said, the smile evident in his voice. "I like redheads myself."

"Really?" It was her turn to smile. "And how

many redheads have you ever—'' She stopped, hesitating about what to call what they had together.

"Only one," he said. "If you don't count Miss Hazel."

"Who is Miss Hazel?"

"My second-grade teacher—though as I look back I suspect hers came from a bottle. I was madly in love with her. She married during spring break and broke my heart."

"Poor baby."

"I recovered. And I discovered baseball about that time. Say, could I interest you in lunch or dinner tomorrow?"

"I'd love to say yes, but Mondays are always murder in the office, and Tuesday doesn't look much better. Could we shoot for Wednesday instead?"

"If that's the best we can do," he said. "Give me a call if you find some extra time."

"It's a deal. Good night, Cole."

"Good night, Red."

"Don't call—'' But he'd already hung up.

Was it her imagination or did he sound a little pissed that they couldn't get together tomorrow? She shrugged. Sooner or later the time demands of being a doctor always got in the way of her relationships. She sliced off a wedge of apple and dipped it into the jar of peanut butter. A shame, but that's the way of the world. And that was why, she told herself, she needed to guard her heart carefully.

When she finished her make-do supper, she watched the news, then flicked off the TV and the light. Sleep didn't come easily. Her mind was a jumble of Cole Outlaw and the hospice project and a worrisome patient or two and Christmas plans with her folks and…Cole Outlaw.

After tossing and turning for several minutes, she resorted to relaxation exercises: imagining that she was on a sunny beach, tensing and releasing muscle groups starting with her toes and working up her body.

By the time she reached her shoulders, the tension had melted away and she was drifting…drifting… drifting—

A noise snatched her from the reverie. Her eyes flew open. She tensed anew, straining to listen.

There, she heard it again. Like the low creak of a rusty cellar door being shoved open.

Her breath caught and her heart almost bolted from her chest.

She didn't have a cellar door. She didn't even have a cellar.

Someone was in the house!

Had she locked up?

Yes, of course. She remembered locking the door behind her and setting the alarm.

She sat up but didn't turn on a lamp. The night-light cast a dim illumination over the room, enough to see that the cats were missing from her bed. Had they gotten into something?

Of course. That was it.

She was going to skin those two, she thought as she tossed back the covers and got out of bed.

The low grating sound came again.

Grabbing a heavy pewter candlestick just in case, she stole quietly from the room and tiptoed in the direction of the noise, the hall night-lights guiding her way. She stopped outside the guest-room door, senses on high alert, straining to listen.

Could she hear breathing or was it her imagination?

The cats?

Too adenoidal for the cats.

Her nose tickled. Lord, she couldn't sneeze now. Clamping her nostrils shut, she waited until the urge passed.

When it was gone, she peeked around the open door.

A large lump was mounded under the bedcovers. Her pulse kicked into overdrive.

The candlestick held high, she flipped on the overhead light and strode to the bed shouting, "What are—"

Cats yowled and scattered. The lump shot up screaming bloody murder, flailing and yelling, "Lord, save me!"

"Gladys! What are you doing here?"

"Don't hit me, Dr. Kelly. Don't hit me."

Kelly lowered the candlestick. "I'm not going to hit you. What are you doing here?"

Gladys began to wail and babbled, "I was cold, freezing cold, and I couldn't get warm no way I tried, and Homer was passed out with the bedroom door locked, and I came here but you was gone, and I didn't have no place to go so I let myself in, and I was trying to get warm and I got sleepy."

"Gladys, slow down. Why were you so cold?" She handed the housekeeper a tissue.

"'Cause the gas company shut our heat off, and I didn't have nothing to wrap up in 'cept a tablecloth."

After a big honking blow, Gladys said, "Dr. Kelly, are you mad at me?"

"I don't know. I'm still trying to recover from being terrified. You scared me half to death."

"Not any worse than you scared me," Gladys said, slapping her hand across her ample bosom. "I thought you was Homer come to bash me for good."

"When are you going to leave that man?"

"Homer? I couldn't leave him. I vowed before God that I'd stick by him, and I aim to. He didn't mean no harm. He just went out with his brother, and that no good Delbert got to him to drinkin' and we had some words, and he locked hisself in the bedroom. I shouldn't agot on to him so, but it being Sunday and all, my bad nature just come up on me."

"Gladys—" Kelly gritted her teeth, knowing from past experience that trying to convince Gladys to leave her sorry husband was futile. In any case, now was not the time to discuss it.

"Dr. Kelly, my heart's apalpitatin' something awful. I believe it's angina pectoreemus. I may be dying."

"That's angina pectoris, and I don't think you have it. You've just been frightened and upset."

"Would you check to be sure?"

Kelly went to the den and got her bag.

After listening to Gladys's chest and her back and thumping around for good measure, she asked several professional-sounding questions, then pronounced her free from angina. She shook out an antacid from the unmarked bottle in her bag and handed it to Gladys. "Take this. It will help you sleep. And I'll see that your gas is turned back on tomorrow."

"Oh, thank you, Dr. Kelly. I don't know what I'd do without you. I was afraid you were going to kick me out in the cold."

"Not tonight. But, Gladys, you are never again to come into the house without my permission. You frightened me. What if I had called police or bashed your head in?"

"I'm awful sorry, Dr. Kelly."

Kelly went back to her room and got into bed. Peanut butter and apple warred in her stomach. She took a couple of antacids herself before she turned off the light. Why did she put up with Gladys's shenanigans?

Because she was a sucker, of course.

ON WEDNESDAY AFTERNOON Kelly had planned to put up her Christmas tree, and that morning Gladys had brought down all the boxes from the apartment over the garage that she used for storage. They were sitting in the den waiting for her attention when she got home from her half day at the office. But instead of decorating, she put on jeans and a sweater and met Cole for lunch at the Twilight Tearoom.

He looked very handsome in his new khakis and sweater. The sweater had a lovely stormy gray pattern, and the color matched his eyes exactly, eyes that seemed to be on her every time she looked up from her plate, eyes that seemed to devour her with the same relish as his food. She squirmed and tried to eat her salad. What was it about this man that set her tingling all over?

Silly question. Sex appeal oozed from him and revved up her libido like crazy. If everyone in town wouldn't have suspected exactly what was going on, she would have liked nothing better than to spend the afternoon in his apartment. In his bed. Unfortunately the domino players would have gotten an earful.

After lunch they decided on her second choice—to drive to Travis Lake to see a movie.

A chick flick or a blood-and-guts guy film? At the theater they had a hard time deciding between the two, and nothing else particularly appealed to either of them.

"I'll let you pick," Cole said.

"No way. We'll flip a coin."

The romantic comedy won.

Inside, he bought popcorn and stuck the box in a side pocket of his walker. She carried the soft drinks. There weren't more than a dozen other people in the small theater, so they found good seats on the aisle about halfway down.

To Cole's credit, he didn't grumble about the sappy scenes nor did he fall asleep. He put his arm around her and fed her popcorn while she sat enthralled. And when she sniffed a bit in a touching moment, she glanced at him. He smiled and winked and squeezed her hand.

What a sweetheart he was.

When the music came up and The End flashed on the screen, he leaned over and kissed her on the cheek. "Cute movie. Did you enjoy it?"

She nodded. "I really did. I don't come to the movies very often. This was fun. Want to go see the other one now?"

"I don't think so. I need to move around some. How about we rent a DVD instead? We can go back to my place and watch it and make out." He wiggled his eyebrows.

She smiled. "Sounds like a winner to me."

THEY SPENT a fair amount of time in the video section of Bullock's Grocery picking out a guy movie that Cole wanted to see. When they arrived at the Twilight Inn, the domino bunch were just closing down their game in the office.

"We're going to watch a DVD," Cole said to them, patting the disk case in his walker pocket.

"That so," Curtis said, winking at Howard.

"Enjoy yourselves," Howard said, winking at B.D.

B.D. smiled as he stowed the folded card table behind the desk and pulled on a heavy plaid jacket. "Well, we'd best be gettin' along."

"A DVD?" Will scratched his head. "Best I recall—"

"Will," Curtis said, "you ain't recalled nothing right since 1973. Let's get out of these young folks' way." He put the domino box in a drawer and shooed the others out of the office.

Inside the apartment, Kelly shrugged off her jacket and said, "How about I make some coffee?"

"Great. I'll get the DVD set up."

Kelly was still measuring the grounds when Cole said, "Uh...we've got a problem."

"What's that?"

"No DVD player."

She finished with the coffeemaker, then went to stand beside him and frown at the TV. "Didn't you know?"

"Obviously not," he said. "I guess I was thinking

about home. I've only watched regular TV since I've been here. Sorry. I feel like a fool."

"No problem. We can go to my place to watch the movie."

"I don't have anybody to cover the desk or the phone," he said, slipping his arms around her waist and pulling her close. "How 'bout we forget the movie part and just stay here and make out."

"A splendid idea. Want coffee first?"

"Later," he said, brushing his lips against hers. "Much later." He outlined her mouth with the tip of his tongue. "You taste salty."

"It's the popcorn. From the movie."

He licked her mouth with a long swipe. "Delicious," he murmured before he teased her lips apart and kissed her deeply.

She melted against him and thrilled at the urgency of his exploration, using her tongue as he used his. His hands slipped beneath her sweater to touch her skin, and his fingers flicked open the hooks of her bra.

Her cell phone rang.

Her damned cell phone rang.

"Ignore it," he said, nuzzling her neck and stroking her breast.

She sucked back a gasp at the delicious sensation. "I can't. I have to answer it." Managing to pull away, she answered on the third ring.

It was her service. An emergency.

"I have to go," she said, hooking her bra and straightening her sweater. "Don't be angry."

"I'm not angry," he said. "Frustrated as the devil, but not angry. Can you come back later?"

"I'll try," she said. "It may be late."

"I'm not going anywhere."

Chapter Eight

Things got hairy after Kelly left Cole, and she wasn't even able to call him until after nine o'clock on Wednesday night. She didn't have much time to talk then. It was almost eleven when she got home, fed the cats and warmed up a helping from the tuna casserole Gladys had left in the fridge.

The casserole was ghastly. And Thursday morning she felt a little queasy when she got up. No wonder. She'd have been better off not eating at all. She hated tuna. It reminded her of cat food. Did anybody really eat the stuff? she wondered as she dumped the rest of the awful-smelling concoction down the garbage disposal. If she hadn't been starving when she got home, she wouldn't have eaten it at all.

One of these days, she was going to have to order Gladys never to make the vile mess again. Subtle hints hadn't done the job.

She quickly made a piece of toast, smeared it with peanut butter and ate it as she drove to the office for a staff meeting. The rest of her day was busy as usual. She'd tried to phone Cole at lunchtime, but he was out, and that evening, she'd only had time to poke her head in for a moment on her way to aerobics class. Friday wasn't much better. She'd awakened with indigestion again and vowed to improve her eating habits, then spent a busy day and ended up having dinner at midnight.

Saturday she absolutely had to put up the tree and decorations and shop for groceries. Christmas was the following week, and half the gifts she'd bought were still to be wrapped. She considered inviting Cole over for dinner, but by the time she finished her chores, she was tired and fell asleep on the couch.

When the phone rang, Kelly was so out of it that for a minute she couldn't remember where she was. Odd. She was usually instantly awake and alert. Grabbing it on the third ring, she mumbled, "Hello."

"Did I wake you?" Cole asked.

"No problem. I must have overdosed on holly and tinsel. I usually don't nap in the daytime."

"You've been a busy girl. I was going to invite you to dinner tonight if you're free."

She glanced at her watch, but it was missing. "What time is it?"

"Four forty-eight. Don't you accept late dates?"

Smiling, she said, "Are you asking me for a date?"

"Yep. But either you'll have to drive or I'll have to ask my dad to chauffeur us. He and Mom will handle night duty here. I thought we might drive over to Travis Lake and have a nice dinner out. Are you on call this weekend?"

"No, it's Dr. Ridge's turn. And I'd love to have dinner. How does Mexican food sound? I feel like I could eat a dozen tamales."

"Sounds good to me," Cole said. "What time?"

"I'll pick you up about six-thirty."

Kelly hurried to put away the wrapping paper and ribbon, then take a nice long bubble bath. She even put on some slightly decadent underwear that she'd bought last summer on a whim and chose a corn-flower-blue silk blouse to wear with her wool pants and blazer. While the look was tailored, she felt downright sexy with the sensual fabrics next to her skin and knowing that her bra and panties were mere scraps of silk and soft lace that matched her blouse.

She unbuttoned another button of her blouse and was humming as she reached for her car keys.

AMUSED, Cole watched Kelly as she peeled the corn shuck from another tamale and put the wrapper onto the pile on a side plate.

She glanced up and caught him watching her. "What?"

"Want another dozen?"

Grinning, she said, "Don't tempt me. I told you I had a yen for tamales."

"I have a yen for something else."

"What? Aren't your enchiladas good?"

"Very good, but I was thinking of you." He took her finger that she was about to lick and licked it himself. Very slowly.

Her eyes met his. "Don't distract me," she said. "I have two more to go." But she didn't pull her hand away. Nor her gaze.

"Sorry." He let go of her. "Finish your tamales."

"I couldn't eat another bite."

"How about sopapillas?"

"With honey?"

He nodded.

She brightened. "I've suddenly found room."

He laughed. He'd never before thought of a doctor as adorable. But that's what she was: adorable. And beautiful. And sexy as hell. All evening he'd been mesmerized by her cleavage and by the occasional flash of blue lace that matched her blouse. He wanted his hands on her in the worst way. He'd been lying awake nights thinking of her, anticipating their next time together.

He wanted to say, "Forget the damned sopapillas, and let's go home and get in the sack." But he didn't. Instead he ordered the dessert and watched as she drizzled honey over the puffs of fried dough, fantasizing pouring honey over her body and licking it off. Instead he settled for her fingers again.

"If you keep doing that," she said, "I'll never get these eaten." She leaned closer and whispered, "And the guy at the next table is getting bug-eyed watching."

"Want me to punch his lights out?"

She laughed. "Not hardly."

Finally she finished, and he paid the check.

As they went to the car, Kelly said, "I've noticed how much better you're walking. The physical therapy must be working."

"It is. Dan Robert says I'm his star pupil. He thinks that in a couple of weeks I can graduate from the walker to a cane, and he swears that I'll be almost as good as new in a couple of months and could think about going back to work."

"And you're eager to do that?"

"I'm champing at the bit. I'm not cut out for idleness in a small town. I'd go nuts. If I were healthy, I'd be out of here like a shot.''

The drive back to the Twilight Inn seemed to take forever, and when they went in his folks were watching a movie on the DVD player that J.J. had loaned him. He wanted to kick them out, but he could hardly do that. In fact, his dad shushed him when he started to talk. The pair of them were engrossed.

''You'll enjoy this, son,'' Wes said, never taking his eyes from the screen. ''It hasn't been started too long, and it's great. I've been wanting to see this. This guy is an undercover cop on to a major drug deal in San Francisco, and he's tougher than an old wild boar. Sit down. Sit down.''

''Maybe we should run along, Wes,'' Miss Nonie said.

''No, no,'' Kelly said. ''Stay and enjoy the movie.''

Cole could have throttled her. He sat down in his recliner, and Kelly sat on the couch with his mom and dad. What a way to spend their evening. When his folks turned back to the TV, he looked at Kelly and rolled his eyes. She merely smiled and gave a slight shrug. He glanced at her a few moments later and saw her eyes drooping; he caught himself dozing once or twice himself.

Sometime later he awoke with his dad shaking him. He sat up and looked around the room for Kelly. She was gone. ''Where'd she go?''

''Dr. Kelly? She left about half an hour ago,'' his dad said. ''She didn't even want to stay and see the end of the movie.''

''She seemed awfully tired,'' Miss Nonie added.

"She said she'd had a busy week and needed to get home before she fell asleep. Fact is, she dropped off a time or two, same as you. Son, are you getting enough rest? Maybe staying here and watching over this place by yourself is too much for you. There's always a room with us, you know."

"I'm fine, Mama. And, believe me, I get plenty of rest around here. No need for you to worry."

"It's a mother's prerogative to worry." She gave him a peck on the cheek. "We'll be running along now. It was awfully sweet of Dr. Kelly to take you on an outing, wasn't it?"

"Very sweet," he said, trying his best to smile as he ground his teeth.

His dad picked up his hat and said, "Anytime you want us to lend a hand here, son, just give us a call."

"I'll do that, Dad."

When his folks were safely away, he let out a string of oaths and slammed the paperback by his chair onto the floor. Then he picked up the book and hurled it across the room, bouncing it off the wall. Frustration didn't begin to describe what he felt.

He considered calling Kelly, but if it was true that she was tired, she was probably in bed by now. Alone. He couldn't believe he'd fallen asleep on her. Or that his folks had hung around. He cursed some more and paced—and it was damned hard to pace with a walker.

SITTING IN CHURCH on Sunday morning, Kelly felt the hair on the back of her neck prickle. She glanced over her left shoulder and saw Cole with his brother Frank and the twins. He winked at her. She winked back,

then turned around before old Mrs. Modisette
thumped her on the head. Mrs. Modisette was a
thumper who brooked no cutting up in church—from
child or adult.

When the service was over she found Cole and his
niece Janey outside waiting for her.

"Frank has gone to get the car. I'm having Sunday
dinner with them, and you're invited. If you like hot
dogs."

"We're having a weenie roast," Janey said.

"Isn't it a little chilly for a weenie roast?" she
asked.

"We're roasting them in the fireplace," the five-
year-old told her. "Please come, Dr. Kelly. Please,
please, please. I'll cook your weenie. I never get them
all black like Jimmy does."

"I would love to come, but I already have plans.
Could I have a rain check?"

"Sure," Janey said. "What's a rain check?"

"It's a way of saying that I'd like to be invited
another time."

"When it's raining?"

"No, that's just a figure of speech."

"What's a— There's Daddy and Jimmy. Bye, Dr.
Kelly." Janey raced off.

As Kelly walked with Cole toward Frank's car, he
said, "Sorry I zonked out on you last night. I couldn't
believe that my folks stayed."

She chuckled. "I don't imagine they had a clue
about our plans. But don't worry about it, I was about
to fall asleep myself. Sorry that I can't make it for
the weenie roast, but one of my patients is celebrating
her hundredth birthday today, and I promised to join

in the luncheon festivities. Want to come to dinner at my house tonight?''

"Sure. I'll find someone else to baby-sit the motel office.''

"I'll pick you up at six-thirty.''

BY SIX-FIFTEEN, the stuffed pork roast was in the oven baking, the fruit salad made and in the fridge, the side dishes done and waiting to be reheated, and the rolls were ready to pop in the oven when they returned. Tantalized by the smells, Rocky and Pierre were in the kitchen twining around her ankles.

"This is people food, boys. I'm having company tonight and don't make pests of yourselves.''

They promised nothing.

She made a last minute check of the small table she'd set up in front of the fireplace where the logs were ready to be lit. Sparkling crystal and silver sat atop the red cloth, and a centerpiece she'd made of fresh pine and holly and shiny gold balls held tall red candles. Very festive…and intimate, she thought with a smile.

By six twenty-nine, she had driven to the Twilight Inn and parked beside a motorcycle in front of the office. At six-thirty on the dot, she knocked on the apartment door.

The door opened almost immediately. "You're prompt," Cole said.

"Try to be.''

"Come in and let me get my jacket. This is Trip. His grandfather, Howard, is one of the guys who works here during the day.''

A lanky kid about eighteen or so unfolded from the

couch. He had assorted body piercings and two-toned hair from a bad bleach job. ''Ma'am,'' he said, giving her a nod.

''It may be late when I get back,'' Cole told Trip.

''Knock yourself out. I'll sack out on the couch if I get sleepy.''

On their way to the car, Cole said, ''I hope that punk doesn't make off with the family silver while I'm gone.''

Kelly laughed. ''What family silver?''

''Amend that to J.J.'s DVD player.''

''I wouldn't worry. I know his mother, and underneath that exterior is a decent interior. He's an honor student at Texas Tech. Biology, I think.''

''Looks like a street punk to me,'' Cole said.

''Being a policeman has jaded you. Even a lot of regular kids look pretty strange these days. I cringe when some of my younger patients come in with wild assortments of large tattoos, but all I can do is hope the needles were clean. I wonder sometimes how they'll feel about their body art when they're grandparents.''

''Me, too,'' he said. ''I must be getting old.''

''Don't remind me. I don't even recognize most of the bands the young people listen to nowadays, and I used to be able to name the top ten songs and sing the lyrics.''

Instead of helping him into the car, she let him manage stowing the walker and getting in on his own while she got behind the wheel. He did fine.

Once inside, he leaned over and kissed her briefly. ''Thanks.'' He nuzzled her neck. ''Um. You smell good. Like cinnamon and sugar.''

"Must be dessert you're smelling."

"Why don't we skip dinner and go straight to dessert." He playfully nipped her ear.

"Down, boy. We have to eat first to keep up our strength. And I have to get home before our food burns. You like pork roast?"

"I like anything except pigs' feet and cauliflower." He nuzzled some more and circled her inner ear with his tongue.

"Buckle your seat belt and let's leave, or we'll be the talk of the town tomorrow."

When he moved away, she took a deep breath and started the car. Her inner motor was revved up more than all those horses under her hood. And her foot was a little heavy as she drove home.

"Hope you don't mind if I bring you in the back way," she said.

"Not at all. You have a pretty place here. I like your patio. You ever use that fire pot?"

"The chiminea? I haven't yet, but I keep meaning to. It was a birthday gift." She opened the back door and held it wide while he easily managed the two steps up into the den. "Come in. *Mi casa, su casa.*"

The cats came running and immediately began winding around her legs and his. Cole looked startled.

"Back off, guys," Kelly said to the cats. "Don't trip our guest. Cole, these rude fellows are Rocky and Pierre. The one with the ragged ear is Rocky."

"You have *cats?*"

"What's the matter, don't you like cats?" she asked as she turned on the gas to light the logs in the fireplace.

"Uh, I like them okay, I guess. I'm more of a dog person myself."

She lit the candles on the table. "I always have been, too, but I don't have time to give a dog proper attention. These guys sort of adopted me, and they're pretty self-sufficient. I'll put them in the guest room."

"No, no," he said. "That's not necessary."

"Make yourself comfortable," she told him, gesturing toward the couch. "Let me check the roast, then I'll pour the wine."

"I'm allowed wine?"

She smiled. "It's nonalcoholic, but we can pretend to get a buzz."

"I've got a buzz already, and I haven't even touched the stuff." The cock of his eyebrow bordered on lecherous as he took her into his arms and kissed her.

His mouth was greedy, and for a moment she gave herself over to the mind-blowing sensation. Then she pushed him away. "Down, boy. I worked my delicate fingers to the bone fixing this meal, and I don't intend to let it burn. Sit down and cool off. I'll be right back."

He didn't sit down. He and the cats followed her into the kitchen. "Smells good in here." He sat on a stool at the island while she washed her hands.

"Thanks," she said as she peeked into the oven. The tenderloin looked perfect. She took it out and put it on the counter to rest before slicing, slipped the rolls into the oven to bake and the roasted new potatoes in to finish browning.

Cole sneezed.

"*Gesundheit!*" She plucked a tissue from the box

on the shelf and handed it to him, then turned the pot of green beans on low to reheat.

"Thanks."

"No problem. Will you pour our wine?" she asked, setting the bottle on the table.

"Sure." While he was pouring he sneezed again.

"Are you getting a cold?"

"Hope not." He blew his nose.

By the time they'd drunk a glass of faux wine and the food was ready to serve, he'd sneezed twice more. She touched his forehead. "You don't seem feverish."

"I'm fine. Boy, this looks good," he said as she served their food from the island.

With Rocky trailing behind her and Pierre close beside Cole, she carried their plates to the table by the fireplace. On the way Cole had another bout of sneezing. When they sat down, she noticed that his eyes were watering, and he'd started wheezing slightly.

"Cole, are you allergic to anything?"

He shrugged slightly and picked up his fork. "Some perfumes." He took a bite of the tenderloin. "This is fantastic."

"What else?"

"Best I've ever had. You're a great cook."

Exasperated, she said, "I wasn't fishing for more compliments. I meant what else are you allergic to?"

He looked pained. "Cats."

Chapter Nine

"Cats! Damnation!" Kelly said, jumping to her feet. "Get up and get your coat on."

"Are you throwing me out?"

"I'm getting you out of the house until I can do something with the cats. Do you have medication?"

"Not with me," Cole said as she grabbed his coat.

"We'll go back to the motel and get it."

"No, I meant not with me in Naconiche. It's at home. My place in Houston."

Once outside on the patio, she said, "I'll see if I can find something here. Why didn't you tell me sooner that you were allergic to cats? I could have put them up."

"I didn't know you had cats, and by the time I found out, it was late. I didn't want to ruin your evening."

She rolled her eyes and bit her tongue to keep from commenting on the male ego. "I'll be right back."

Charging back inside, she caught Rocky on the table sniffing at her plate and swishing his tail frighteningly close to a lighted candle. "Scat!" She clapped her hands.

Rocky scrambled for a footing, then shot off the table and, in three bounds, leaped to the top of the tall bookcase. She caught the candlestick as it toppled and blew out the flame. She wasn't so lucky with the wineglass. She ignored the spill for the moment and went searching for allergy medication.

Luckily she found a sample in the bottom of her medical bag. She grabbed a freshly laundered quilt from the linen closet and a glass of water on her way out the door.

"Here," she said, handing him the cap and the water.

"This is the same stuff I have at home," he said. "It works pretty well."

"I'm really sorry about the cats. Wrap up in this quilt while I go inside and stow them in the guest room."

"It's not *that* cold," he said. "I'm not likely to freeze."

"Humor me. That furniture is likely to be chilly on the tush. I'll be right back."

The cats had other ideas.

No matter how much she cajoled, begged or demanded, Rocky wouldn't budge from his perch atop the bookcase. Pierre had taken up residence under the couch. She got on her hands and knees on the floor and tried to reach him, but her arm wasn't long enough. She resorted to a broom to drag him out. He thought it was a great game and skittered from one end of the couch to the other.

After fifteen minutes of futile effort, Kelly was sweating and frustrated. She should have known better. Cats always won.

Maybe if she gave them a few minutes alone, they would leave their places and she could catch them. Taking along the butane fire lighter, she went outside where she found Cole sitting bundled up on the swing.

"Sorry, but the cats aren't cooperating right now. It may take a few minutes to round them up, so I thought I'd light the chiminea. Or would you rather go to the hamburger place and get something to eat?"

"I sort of had my mouth set for some of that great dinner you cooked," he said.

This wasn't the romantic evening she planned, she thought as she tossed some kindling and pine needles into the fire pot and lit them. After the kindling caught, she added some small lengths of dry wood and soon a nice blaze was going.

Shooting Cole a grin, she beat her chest with a fist. "Me, woman. Make fire."

He chuckled. "You're a woman of many talents."

"Oh, I don't know. I seem to be lousy at herding cats. How are you feeling?"

"Fine. I can probably go back inside."

"Let's not chance it just yet, especially until I corral the critters. Hang with me, I'll be back in a sec."

Inside she found Rocky on the table again, but when she grabbed for him, he was back atop the bookcase faster than a speeding bullet. Heaven only knew where Pierre was.

"Come down from there this instant!" she ordered.

Rocky yawned.

"If you don't come down, I'll taking you to the SPCA first thing in the morning, buster."

He didn't believe a word of her threat. He grinned and lifted his leg to lick.

She got the broom again and stood on a chair, intending to sweep him from the ledge. As she swept, Rocky leaped from the bookcase onto the top of her newly decorated Christmas tree and rode it down as it crashed to the floor. A limb caught the red tablecloth on her intimate table and dragged off cloth, plates and all. Shiny balls and glass birds flew in every direction, some shattering amid the cold pork tenderloin and potatoes and green beans.

She dropped the broom, stood poker straight and took three deep breaths. Someday she might think this was funny.

It wasn't funny now.

Without a word, she strode to the kitchen, prepared two more plates of food and nuked them. Loading everything on a tray, she marched outside to the patio.

Cole looked puzzled when he saw her and was about to open his mouth.

"Don't ask," she said, sitting on the bench beside him. "We're dining al fresco. Consider it an adventure."

The rest of the evening went downhill from there. The meat was dry, the green beans were mush and the potatoes chilled rock-hard before they could eat two bites. Being a gentleman, Cole complimented the meal, but she noticed that he didn't eat very much. Neither did she. It was hard to eat with her teeth chattering and her nose numb.

He must have noticed her turning blue because he set aside his plate and hers and pulled her to him. "Come cuddle under the quilt with me," he said, bundling the cover around both of them. "You look like you're about to freeze."

"It is a bit nippier than I thought." Wrapping her arms around him, she put her head on his shoulder and snuggled as close as she could get, and he hugged her to the warmth of his body. The chiminea needed more wood, but she wasn't about to leave her cocoon to add any. She burrowed closer and glanced up at the sky. "Look at all the stars. Aren't they beautiful?"

"Yes, they are. There's the Big Dipper. I can't remember the last time I noticed it."

"Me, either, but I remember, as a kid, spending hours watching stars and finding the constellations."

"Did you have a telescope?" he asked.

She nodded. "I got one for Christmas when I was twelve."

"Me, too. I don't know whatever happened to it."

"Mine is still in my old room at my folks' house."

He touched his forehead against hers, then rubbed her nose against his. "Your nose is cold."

"You should feel it from this side. It feels like an ice cube. Cole, I'm really sorry about the awful dinner and—"

"The dinner was just fine."

"You didn't eat very much."

"I'm saving room for dessert," he said.

He kissed her, but his lips were as cold as hers were.

"I have an idea," she said. "I'll get the apple dumplings, and we can go to your place to have dessert."

"Excellent idea."

She loaded the remains of their dinner back on the tray, stashed it inside on the kitchen counter and grabbed the dessert dish.

Problem was, when they got to the Twilight Inn they found Trip on the couch—sound asleep and snoring. Worse, they couldn't rouse him.

"I wonder if he's been into my pain pills," Cole said.

"Check the bottle."

He got the bottle from his nightstand, and they counted. None seemed to be unaccounted for.

Kelly raised the kid's lids and peered into his eyes. "I think he's just zonked out in deep sleep."

"Big help he'd be if somebody needed a room while we were gone."

"Let's warm up the dessert. Maybe the smell of food will rouse the lazy little punk."

It didn't. Trip didn't so much as roll over.

"Tell you what," Cole said, "let's throw a sheet over him and go make out in the bedroom."

"I can't do that. What if he woke up at an awkward moment and found me—us—?"

"Let him get his own girl."

"No way, tiger. His mother is my Sunday-school teacher. Are there any vacant rooms?"

"Number three is empty," he said, grinning.

But when they went to get the key, it was gone from the box. In its place was a registration card.

"Mr. and Mrs. Alton Frederick from Amarillo," he read. "Trip must have stayed awake long enough to rent the unit. Looks like there's no more room at the inn."

Kelly groaned. "Bad pun." She kissed his cheek.

"This doesn't seem to be working out, and I need to go home and clean up the mess the cats made."

"Why don't I just drag Trip out by his heels and throw him over his motorcycle?"

She laughed. "Why don't we try this again next weekend?"

"Is it going to be a week before I see you again?"

"Maybe not, but my folks are coming for the holidays, and I need to spend time with them."

He took her into his arms and kissed her with a heat and urgency that left her panting.

"Think that will hold you for a week?" he asked.

"Probably not." She drew his head down and kissed him again.

BY THE TIME Kelly got home, she was exhausted, and she dreaded to face the disaster in her living room. To heck with it, she thought as she crossed the patio. She'd get up early in the morning and help Gladys clear the mess.

The quilt she'd brought out earlier still lay in a heap on the swing.

She started to pick it up on her way in when the heap moved. Kelly gave a shriek and jerked back.

Gladys jumped up from where she'd huddled beneath the quilt. "Oh, praise the Lord, Dr. Kelly. I'm glad to see you. I was about to freeze."

Her hand splayed over her pounding heart, Kelly said, "Gladys, what on earth are you doing here?"

"It's Homer. He— Oh, the shame of it. It's too awful to speak of. I've left for good, but I didn't have anywhere to go at this hour of the night. There isn't even a room to rent anywhere in town. I'm throwing myself on your mercy."

Kelly sighed. She wasn't in the mood for Gladys's biweekly histrionics over that louse she married, but she said, "Come on in. You can sleep in the guest room tonight."

"Oh, thank you, thank you. I'll make some other arrangements tomorrow. I swear I will."

"Fine, fine. Come on in. I'm too tired to think about it now."

Kelly trudged inside with Gladys on her heels.

"Blessed be, Dr. Kelly! Robbers have looted your house. Call the police!"

"Robbers didn't do this. The cats did."

"I can't believe those sweet babies did such a thing." Gladys bent to stroke the two rogues that purred and twined themselves around Gladys's ankles.

"Believe it. I'm going to bed. We can clean up this mess in the morning."

KELLY FELT like death warmed over the next morning, but she dragged herself into the shower and dressed. She dreaded facing the disaster in the living room, but Gladys, bless her sweet heart, was already up and everything was tidy.

"Place was in a terrible scramble. Did you and your gentleman friend get into a fight?" Gladys asked.

"Certainly not. And to what gentleman friend are you referring?"

"Sheriff Wes and Miss Nonie's oldest boy, the one that got shot up in Houston. I've heard tell that you and him are keeping company. He's a handsome devil, all right, but you've got to watch out for them good-looking ones or they'll break your heart. Just consider Homer.''

Kelly muffled her snort of laughter with a cough. Homer was a scarecrow with an underslung jaw, a beak of a nose and several missing teeth. "I'm not likely to get my heart broken. We're just friends.''

"Uh-huh,'' Gladys said, as if she didn't believe a word of it. "How about some eggs and sausage and—''

"Just toast. Dry.''

"Now, Dr. Kelly, you're got to eat more breakfast than that. You should know that it's the most important meal of the day, and you need to keep up your strength for doctoring. How about some nice pancakes and bacon?''

"*Toast.*''

"Okay, okay. You're the doctor. But I'm gonna make you one of my tuna casseroles for your dinner tonight.''

The thought of tuna casserole made her gag. This was the perfect opening. "Gladys—''

Gladys turned from the sink and smiled so sweetly that Kelly didn't have the heart.

"I—uh—I'm eating out tonight.''

"With that feller of yours, I betcha.''

"I don't have a feller.''

"Deny it all you want, but I've noticed that new glow you've got. I remember that feeling that I had twenty-three years ago when Homer—'' Gladys turned back to the sink. "That all died last night when

Homer brought his bimbo into our home.'' Her voice broke.

"Oh, Gladys, he didn't.''

"He did. God's truth, I thought I was going to die.''

Kelly rubbed the sniffing woman's back. "I'm so sorry.''

"The scales finally fell from my eyes when he done that. I've seen the last of that man. There's no more forgiveness left in me.''

"Is there anything I can do?''

"No, but thank you just the same. I made up my mind during the night that I'm not going to let Homer and his sinful ways run me from my home. Soon as I finish up here, I'm going to go back to the house and kick his sorry ass—and his floozies—out the door.''

"Need any help?''

Gladys laughed. "With the fire I got in my belly I can handle it just fine. Don't you worry one bit about it. You'd better get along or you're going to be late.'' She handed her a sack from the fridge.

"What's this?''

"A snack for later. Some of that nice fruit salad I found in the icebox.''

"I forgot all about it last night.''

Kelly had a spring in her step when she crossed the patio to her car. While she was sorry that Gladys was hurt, it was past time for Homer and her to split. Good riddance to a louse.

She called Cole on her way to the office. He sounded sleepy when he answered. "Did I wake you?''

"No," he said, "Trip and I were just having breakfast."

She laughed. "Is he still there?"

"Yep. And the kid's a pretty good cook."

"Ordinarily I am, too, but you couldn't prove it by last night's meal. I'm really sorry about the disaster. How about I stop by tonight with hamburgers?"

"Hamburgers?"

"It's either that or tuna casserole," she said.

"I prefer hamburgers."

"A man after my own heart. See you about seven."

She was feeling even better as she strode into her office a couple of minutes later, smiling and greeting her staff.

"You're certainly chipper this morning," her nurse said as she sorted through charts.

"I think I've finally got the Christmas spirit. Jingle bells, jingle bells," she sang as she did a little shuffle. "Who's our first patient?"

"Dixie Russo. But first you need to call J. J. Outlaw at the sheriff's office. He said it was important."

"Did he say what it was about?"

The nurse shook her head. "Just that it was important."

When she called J.J., he skipped the usual pleasantries. "I thought you might want to know that I have to go over and evict Gladys and Homer this morning. I hate to do it, but the rent hasn't been paid in three months, and their landlord's given me no choice."

"Don't you have to serve notice first?" she asked.

"I served the papers to Homer thirty days ago."

"That dirty dog! I'll bet he didn't tell Gladys.

She's going to be devastated.'' Trying quickly to come up with a plan, she drew a blank. ''J.J., can you put off the eviction until this afternoon? I'll see if I can't work out something. Who is the landlord?''

''Warren Iverson.''

Her heart sank. Wouldn't you know?

Chapter Ten

Providence must have scheduled Dixie Russo's checkup that morning. Gladys worked at the Russos' on Tuesdays, so Dixie was concerned when Kelly told her about the impending eviction.

"Any ideas about how we can help her?" Kelly asked.

"Find her a place to live first, then get someone to move her stuff."

"I have an apartment over my garage," Kelly said. "It's only used for storage, but it might do temporarily—but only for Gladys. Homer can find his own place."

"I'll vote for that. That jerk ought to be castrated with a rusty knife. Say, the kid next door is home from college for the holidays, and he has a pickup. I'll enlist him and a couple of his friends to move her."

"Great. If you'll take care of that, I'll pay the boys," Kelly said. "Now who's going to tell Gladys?"

Dixie sighed. "You have patients to see. I guess that leaves me."

"You just earned another star in your crown."

"I don't need another star. I just need a new prescription for birth control pills."

Kelly scribbled on a pad, then tore off and handed the page to Dixie. "There you go."

COLE HAD TO HAVE checked his watch fifty times by the time a tap came on the door at 7:19. Opening it immediately, he found Kelly, sack in hand, looking flagged out.

"Sorry I'm late," she said as she entered. "It's been one of those days. I didn't even have time to shower and change."

"Another minute and I was going to send a posse for you. Tired?"

Nodding as she put the paper bag on the kitchen table, she said, "Worse, my feet hurt." She kicked off her shoes and wiggled her toes.

"There's a great old claw foot tub in the bathroom if you want to take a soak."

"I may take you up on it later, but right now I'm starving. Besides having a Monday of patients— which means a full house—Gladys had a major crisis, which I had to work in." She got paper plates from the cupboard and set out burgers, fries and onion rings. "I hope you like everything on your cheeseburgers."

"I do. Who's Gladys?"

"My maid. Now my tenant." She shook packages of catsup, salt and pepper from the sack onto the table. "Sit. Eat." She tore open the wrappings and took a big bite of her burger. "Oh, that's good. The smell has been driving me crazy since I left the Burger Barn with them. I got malts, too. Chocolate.''

He grinned and joined her at the table while she scarfed down an onion ring and two French fries. ''What was the crisis with Gladys?''

''Well,'' she said between bites, ''J.J. called me this morning and said he had to evict Gladys and Homer, and Dixie went over to my house to tell her and get some kids to move her to the garage apartment.'' She stopped to suck on the straw in her malt.

''Whoa, whoa. Is Dixie their daughter?''

''No, no. Dixie *Russo*. You know her.''

''Oh, Dixie Anderson. What does she have to do with it?''

''Gladys works for Dixie, too. On Tuesdays. She works for Ellen on Thursdays, and for me on Monday, Wednesday and Friday and cleans Noah's and my offices in the evenings.''

''I see,'' he said, trying not to grin again. He'd never seen Kelly quite so hyper. He let her eat in silence for a moment before he said, very slowly, ''And since this is Monday, Gladys was at your house. You called and asked Dixie to handle moving her.''

She stopped midbite and looked at him as if he were crazy. ''No, Dixie was in my office. She volunteered. Sort of. Anyhow, when Dixie and Gladys got to Gladys's house with the college kids and the pickup, Homer and his bimbo had flown the coop, taking most of the furniture, including Gladys's grandmother's antique washstand.''

''Who's the bimbo?''

"I have no idea. Aren't you going to eat?" she asked pointing to his wrapped burger.

"Sure," he said, opening the wrappings and taking a bite. "I'm just fascinated by the mystery of Gladys and the bimbo."

"The bimbo is long gone with Homer, Gladys's husband—who is the world's biggest louse. Anyhow, Gladys had hysterics, fainted and almost scared the college boys to death. I spent my lunch hour reviving her and helping get her moved into the apartment."

"The garage apartment?"

She nodded. "The one over my garage. I've been using it for storage. Of course, there wasn't much to move, not even a bed, so I called Rafferty's Furniture and Ellen. Ellen had an extra refrigerator in her garage, and Florence had an extra couch, as well as a few other things."

"Florence?"

"Dixie's mother-in-law. She did the decorating at Mary Beth and J.J.'s wedding reception."

"So Florence is decorating your garage apartment for the maid?"

Kelly laughed. "I'm babbling, aren't I?"

"A little."

"Anyhow, I left things with them and went back to the office. After my last patient, my nurse helped me clean the offices—I'd told Gladys not to come in—and I made rounds at the hospital, stopped by the Burger Barn and here I am."

"Tired and hungry." He winked. "And your feet hurt."

She patted her tummy. "I'm no longer hungry."

He stood. "I'll be right back." He went into the

bathroom and rummaged around in a basket on the counter until he found a packet of bubble bath and started the water running in the tub. He dumped the packet into the water and sneezed.

"What are you doing?" she asked behind him.

"I'm making you a bubble bath."

She wrapped her arms around his waist and laid her face against his back. "I can't remember anybody ever making a bubble bath for me."

"It's about time they did." He turned and kissed her. "Take off your clothes and get in."

He didn't have to ask her twice. She was already unbuttoning her blouse when he eased out the door.

Cole finished his cheeseburger and malt and cleaned up the mess, then waited another ten minutes before he tapped gently on the bathroom door. "You okay?"

When Kelly didn't answer he cracked the door and looked in. She was sound asleep amid the bubbles. Something squeezed at his heart as he watched her. Somehow, when he wasn't paying attention, she'd gotten under his skin in the worst way. He shook off the feelings. Next thing, he'd be convincing himself he was falling in love, and the chance of a long-term relationship with her was between slim and none. He wasn't going down that road again.

Still, he wished he could pick her up and tuck her in bed. Impossible for a gimp on a walker.

"Kelly," he said softly.

Her eyes popped open, and she glanced around. "I must have dropped off."

"I figured as much when I heard you snoring."

"Do I snore?"

He grinned. "No. Dry off, then come back in the bedroom." He took a little bottle of lotion from the basket before he left.

A couple of minutes later she appeared at the door wearing his robe. He patted the bed and said, "Lie down and put your feet in my lap."

"Are we going to do something kinky?"

He chuckled. "I'm going to give you a foot massage."

"You don't have to do that."

"I know I don't, but I want to." He patted the bed again. "Lie down."

Kelly crawled into bed and stuck her feet on his good leg. When he poured lotion into his hand and began to massage her left foot, she moaned.

"That feels so good," she said.

He worked her arch with his thumbs, and she moaned again. "You're really good at this. I suspect you've had some practice."

"A little. Sharon used to—" *Damn!* He didn't mean to mention her. Nothing could douse an intimate moment like bringing up another woman.

"Your ex-wife?"

"Yeah. She used to have foot cramps from wearing those idiotic spike heels."

"She was nuts to let you go. I'd hang on to you for your massaging skills alone."

"Meaning I have others?"

Her laugh was low and sexy. "Yes. Oh, yes." She wiggled her toes and sighed. "My foot thinks it has died and gone to heaven."

He switched feet, gently kneading the other one from toes to calf for a few minutes. Then his hands stroked farther upward over her knee to her thigh. And higher.

But she was sound asleep.

He didn't have the heart to rouse her. He was rock-hard and wanted her in the worst way, but he'd get over it. She spent her days taking care of everyone else; it was time somebody took care of her. He shucked his clothes, turned off the light and climbed in bed beside her, pulling the covers over them.

She sighed and snuggled against him. His heart swelled like a balloon inside his chest. Kelly Martin was some kind of woman. He was proud to know her.

KELLY AWOKE in a strange bed with a large hairy leg thrown over hers and a hand on her breast. Red numbers on a digital clock said 1:13. For a moment she panicked, then remembered that the hairy leg and the hand belonged to Cole. She hadn't meant to go to sleep, but he was a genius with his fingers. She started to get up, but his arm held her.

"Don't go," he said.

"Are you awake?" she murmured, still half asleep herself.

"Damn right. Who could sleep?" His hand moved from her breast to stroke down her belly and between her legs.

She sucked in a breath and moved with his stroke. "I swear your fingers are magical."

He chuckled and nibbled at her neck. She was raging hot by the time he entered her, and his climax and hers came quickly.

The next thing she knew, she opened her eyes

again and the red numbers on the clock said 5:02.
This time she really did panic.

Dear Lord, she'd spent the entire night with him!

When she tried to get up, Cole held her tightly
against him. "Where are you going?"

"I have to go home before the other half of Naconiche sees my car parked in front of your place."

"What does it matter?"

"Are you kidding?" she asked. "Have you forgotten how people gossip in a small town? I'll probably have a scarlet A painted on my office door. At
the very least every patient I see today will be snick-
ering."

"Tell them you were sitting up with a sick friend,"
he said, grinning.

"Yeah. Sure." She got up, grabbing the robe she'd
lost during the night. "God, my hair is a mess. I must
look like a witch."

Cole raised up on one elbow and watched her.
"Uh-uh. You look like a siren, a sexy wild woman."

Clamping her tangled shock of hair in both hands,
she said, "I'll buy the wild woman part." She twisted
her errant curls into a coil and patted the bed for her
clip.

"Looking for this?" he asked, clicking the clip
open and shut like shark jaws.

She snatched it from him and hurried out of the
room to find her clothes.

They were in a heap on the bathroom floor. Dirty,
but she put them on anyhow and made a face at the
image she saw in the mirror. She'd change when she
got home.

When she came out of the bathroom, Cole was

standing in the kitchenette corner. He'd pulled on a pair of sweatpants, but he was bare-chested, tousled-haired and had a dark shadow of beard. Why did he look so great when she looked so ghastly?

"How about a cup of coffee before you go?" he asked.

"Thanks, but I don't dare. I have to get going." She draped her arms around his neck and kissed him briefly. "Thanks for the foot massage...and the...other."

"You're welcome for the foot massage. As for the other, I think it was mutual." He put his arms around her waist and nipped at her lower lip. "Could I interest you in another...mutual activity before you go?"

"Don't tempt me." She eased from his arms. "I have to go."

It wasn't until she pulled away from the Twilight Inn, the morning still in darkness, that something dawned on her. For the second time they hadn't used any protection. Blast it! She should know better.

It wasn't until she was almost home that it dawned on her why she might be feeling queasy in the mornings.

Chapter Eleven

She was pregnant. Both kits had shown positive.

Of course, sometimes tests registered false positives, and Kelly considered trying a third brand just to be sure, but she'd known even before she'd locked herself in the office bathroom for the urine test. She was pregnant.

Stunned, she sat in her office and stared at the wall. How could it have happened? Well…she knew how it had happened, but how could she have been so careless, so stupid? Not once, but twice.

Of course, the second time wasn't the problem.

Torn between jubilation and despair, she could only sit there feeling numb. She'd planned to begin birth control pills after her next period, but, now that she counted, her next period was well overdue.

What in the world was she going to do?

Should she tell Cole?

Not yet, not yet, a voice inside her said. Was she afraid of what he might say or do? Maybe.

She needed some time first. Things had to sink in, and she had to consider some options. She could just see Warren Iverson now as she waddled along on her rounds nine months pregnant and unmarried; he would go ballistic. And—

Stopping herself from considering all sorts of dire consequences, she took a deep breath and blew it out. Soon patients would be in examining rooms; her parents were arriving in only two days, and she had a million things to do besides her regular load. What was done couldn't be undone, and she simply didn't have time to think about it now.

After the holidays. She'd deal with it after the holidays.

Her nurse tapped on the door. "You have an emergency on line two."

DAYS PASSED IN A BLUR of activity, and before she knew it Kelly's parents arrived in a flurry of hugs and beribboned packages.

"You look tired," her mother said.

"Hush, Normah," her dad said. "She looks great." He put a pile of presents under the tree and backed up to the fire. "Boy, this feels good. It's colder than a witch's—"

"John!"

Her dad only laughed at the admonition. Tall and with a bit of Kelly's red hair still showing in his gray, John Martin was a handsome man with a ready smile and a bit of the devil in his green eyes, which was why his students loved him. And neither Kelly nor her mother was immune to his charm. They both adored him.

"I've missed you guys," Kelly said, hugging her mother again. "How are things at the bank?"

"Busy as usual. There's talk of a merger. I'm not

sure I can survive another one. The good old boys might get me this time.''

''I doubt that,'' Kelly said, knowing that her mother's position as president was secure. Not only was her mother an attractive woman with the good bones of her beauty queen days still strong among the fine lines, but also she was a former Phi Beta Kappa and as tough as a combat boot.

Gladys came bustling in from the kitchen with a tray. ''I've brought coffee and cookies to warm you up.''

''Chocolate chip, I hope,'' John Martin said, his grin wide.

''Yes, sir. I remembered it was your favorite.''

''Hello, Gladys,'' Normah Martin said. ''It's good to see you. How are you?''

''Fine as frog fur after the Lord removed a burden from my life and set me on a new path. By the grace of God I'm living upstairs in Dr. Kelly's garage apartment these days, and things are just dandy. I'll be running along now, but I left a tuna casserole for your supper.''

''Great, great,'' John said, rubbing his hands together. ''Nothing I like better than your tuna casserole.''

When Gladys had gone, Normah rolled her eyes at her husband. ''You must be the only person in the world who can abide that tuna casserole. Kelly, haven't you mustered up the nerve yet to tell her that it's ghastly?''

She laughed. ''I almost made it last week, but I chickened out. Luckily we have an alternative. My friend Carrie has invited us to a potluck dinner party at her fiancé's house tonight if you're up to it.''

"We're always ready for a party," her dad said, dunking a cookie in his coffee. "We can take the casserole."

"You can take the casserole," Kelly said. "I'm taking a salad and peach cobbler."

They spent the afternoon catching up, then gathered the food they were taking and drove to Frank Outlaw's house.

Spotlights illuminated a waving Santa on the front lawn, his sleigh and reindeer made of pine logs and a red bulb blinking on the nose of Rudolph on lead. Icicle lights dripped from the house eaves, and scores of strings of tiny twinkles filled the trees and shrubs.

"This is remarkable," Kelly's dad said as he parked the Lexus behind a black pickup truck. "Sort of reminds me of that Chevy Chase movie."

"It does not, John," her mother said. "There's a line between festive and gaudy, and this doesn't cross it. Almost, but not quite."

Kelly laughed. "Carrie will appreciate hearing that. She and Frank have worked on it for a week or more."

"Now tell me again who Carrie and Frank are," her mother said.

"Carrie is a sorority sister from UT. She's an attorney as well as a landman."

"As in oil?" John asked.

"As in oil. She showed up a few months ago to lease land around here for her uncle's company and ended up engaged to Frank Outlaw, who is the County Court-at-Law judge. Frank is a widower with twins, and he grew up with his brothers and sister in this house. His father was sheriff, and everyone in the family is named after famous outlaws. Most of them will be here, and you'll get it sorted out as we go.''

Garlands of fragrant fresh pine and holly draped the porch railings and were caught up with red velvet bows. More greenery swags and bows draped the entrance, and a huge green wreath with gold balls, glittered pinecones and candy canes hung on the front door.

Carrie swung open the door before Kelly could knock. ''Come in. Come in. Merry Christmas.'' She hugged Kelly and greeted her parents warmly.

Frank was just behind Carrie, smiling and shaking hands after introductions. ''Welcome to Outlaw bedlam,'' he said. ''Let me take your coats.''

After coats were deposited in the hall and food in the kitchen, Frank took Kelly's parents around to introduce them to the clan. Sheriff Wes and Miss Nonie were there, as were J.J., Mary Beth, Katy and the twins.

''Where is the rest of the family?'' Kelly asked Carrie.

''Belle couldn't make it home for the holidays this year, and Sam has gone to pick up Cole.''

''Who's the cute little blonde by the fireplace?''

''Oh, that's Julie, a friend of Sam's,'' Carrie said.

''New romance?''

''I don't know. I'm not quite sure what's going on there, and Sam keeps his cards close to his vest. Come on, let's have some eggnog.''

The front door opened and Sam and Cole entered. She saw Cole scan the room until his eyes rested on

her. Their gazes caught and held. Her breath caught
as well. He smiled. Her legs went wobbly, and she
smiled back.

"Why don't *I* get some eggnog?" Carrie said.

"Whatever."

He made straight for her—and kissed her when he
got there.

"Cole!" she whispered, glancing around.

"I couldn't resist." He chuckled and pointed upward.

They stood underneath a sprig of mistletoe.

"Hey," Sam said, muscling Cole aside. "It's my
turn."

"You do and you die," Cole growled.

Sam only laughed and planted a good one on Kelly.
"It's good to see you, Dr. Darlin'. Did you bring your
folks? Let's go meet them."

"I LIKE YOUR PARENTS," Cole said after they finally
had a moment alone—which was after dessert and
coffee.

"Thanks. I do, too. They're good people."

"Are they staying long?" he asked.

She smiled. "Until Saturday or Sunday. I'm not
sure."

"Good for them. Bad for me. Any chance we could
get together alone?"

"Not much, I'm afraid. I don't get to see them
often, and I'm their only child. As it is I still have to
see patients after Christmas Day. I'll call when they
leave."

He bent close and murmured in her ear, "It can't
be too soon. My dreams are driving me crazy. Think

anyone would notice if we slipped away to my old bedroom?''

A thrill shivered over her at the naughty idea. It was tempting. "They would notice. My mom's giving us the eagle eye as it is."

He nipped at her ear. "Don't you ever like to live dangerously?"

"Down, boy," she said, chuckling. "I'm not an adrenaline junkie like you are."

"Then at least let's go stand under the mistletoe so I can kiss you again."

"Uncle Cole," a small voice said. Jimmy, one of Frank's twins, tugged on Cole's pant leg. "Uncle Cole, can't you make Daddy let us open *one* present tonight? Just *one.* Please?"

Cole smiled indulgently as he looked down at his nephew. "I don't think I can help you there, pardner. He never did like me bossing him around."

"Try, just try," Jimmy begged, tugging Cole's hand.

Kelly smiled. "Give it a shot. We'll be going soon."

Kelly and her parents didn't linger long after that. It had been a tiring day for them, so they said their goodbyes and left.

"I like your young man," her dad said as they drove home.

"Which young man is that?" she asked.

"The Texas Ranger."

"Oh, John," Normah said. "Are you so dense? He's only a tease. It's the older one with the cane who couldn't keep his eyes off her. Cole, isn't that his name, Kelly?"

"Umm."

"Nonie told me the circumstances of his injury. Anything serious going on between the two of you, dear?"

Kelly shrugged. "Maybe."

"I had always thought you might marry another doctor, but I suppose a policeman might do if he's the right one for you. You're not getting any younger, Kelly, and I'm eager to be a grandmother while I still have my faculties."

Kelly's breath caught, and her stomach did a little flip-flop. Amazing how one could push something, even such a significant thing, from the mind, but now her pregnancy loomed in her thoughts. Struggling to keep from blurting out the news, she casually said, "It's not necessary to marry anybody for me to have children."

"No, I suppose that's true nowadays," her mother said, "but a son-in-law would be nice, too."

"I liked Cole," her dad said. "He's a Cowboys fan."

Kelly laughed. Anybody who was a Dallas Cowboys fan was pretty much okay with her father. "I think all the Outlaws are Cowboys fans."

"Nice family."

"Is Cole retiring from police work?" her mom asked.

"I don't know. Probably not. I suspect that he'll return to Houston when his therapy is complete, so don't you two start planning a wedding."

"You wouldn't consider a move?"

"To Houston?" Kelly shook her head. "You know how much I love it here and how much I have invested in my practice and the town. My patients need me, and I couldn't leave the hospice program now that it's in a critical stage. By the way, have I told you the latest about the hospice plans?"

Her father chuckled. "Is that a polite way of changing the subject from our prospects of having grand-children?"

"Yes."

CHRISTMAS WAS LOVELY. They were no emergencies, and her parents adored the gifts she had selected for them—matching cashmere golf sweaters as well as turquoise earrings for her mother and a first edition book that her father had mentioned wistfully. They had given her a forest-green robe that felt heavenly and new black leather driving gloves.

While she was at the office, her mother went antiquing, and her father tagged along to examine the dusty books that were often tucked away in corners, or else he stayed home to work on a scholarly article he was writing. She was so occupied that she didn't think about her pregnancy more than a couple of dozen times.

Her parents left early Sunday morning to beat the traffic, and instead of going to church, Kelly lazed around in her cuddly new robe with her feet up, enjoying the quiet and solitude. Twice she found herself smiling and with her hand resting on her belly—not that there was anything to feel yet.

She was getting used to the idea of having a baby, and she liked it. Of course, one of the many problems would be how and when to tell Cole. He had a right to know, but she wanted to put it off for a while. She was well aware that several things could still go wrong in the first month or so. It was better to wait until she was sure the pregnancy was established before she burdened him with something so serious. Dealing with his injury and recovery was stressful enough for him right now.

Or would he consider her condition a burden?

The subject of parenthood had never come up. He seemed very fond of his nieces and nephew, but that wasn't the same as having to deal 24/7 with one of your own.

For that matter, how was she going to deal with a busy practice and a baby 24/7? Taking a baby to her office didn't seem to be a good option. Every disease in town passed through there.

A nanny, perhaps?

She grinned at the notion of having an English nanny in Naconiche. Oh, well, she had plenty of time to consider solutions.

Shortly after twelve the phone rang.

"What are you doing?" Cole asked.

"Having a cup of yogurt and too many chocolate chip cookies," she answered.

"The soft kind with nuts?"

"Yep."

"My favorite. You still have company?"

"No. My mom and dad went home this morning."

"That new movie you wanted to see is on in Travis Lake, the one with Julia Roberts and what's his name. Interested in driving over to see it this afternoon?"

"Sure. What time?"

They made plans, and suddenly her energy had returned. Due, she decided, to a combination of Cole and chocolate—a luscious and lethal pair of aphrodisiacs. She took a quick shower and dressed, lingering over her lingerie drawer to select something soft and sexy. Amazing how feminine that man made her feel. The cut of her underwear usually didn't enter her mind.

An hour later she drove to the motel wearing black silk and lace under her black pants and sweater and munching on another cookie. She had planned to take the last two cookies to Cole, but she couldn't resist one, and she was eyeing the other with lust in her heart. She'd have Gladys make another batch tomorrow.

He was ready when she rang the bell. He took her in his arms and kissed her.

"I've missed you," he said, kissing her again.

His lips were warm and dangerous. Nobody could kiss the way he did—or turn her on so quickly. She wanted to crawl into his skin. "I've missed you, too. Wanna skip the movie?"

"Excellent idea. There's another one starting in a couple of hours," he said, pulling her inside. "You taste like cookies, and I want to eat you up."

Chapter Twelve

Cole spat out an oath and threw the magazine across the room. He'd been cooped up in this place for nearly two months, and he'd watched about all the television and movies and read all the books and magazines he could tolerate. The thought of another jigsaw puzzle or crossword puzzle drove him up the wall.

He wasn't cut out for the life of an invalid. The only thing that held any interest for him in Naconiche was Kelly, and if it hadn't been for her, he'd have been long gone. But she was working most of the time, and he wasn't. He was still in physical therapy three times a week, but he could get that anywhere. Even a desk job at the department didn't seem so awful now. To ease his boredom, he'd been reduced to sitting in on domino games with the old geezers.

Having a car would help. The doctor had released him to drive for short distances the day before, but his SUV was in Houston and Naconiche didn't have a rental agency. He was tempted to buy a clunker at the used-car lot just to have some wheels.

And why not? He had money in the bank from the

oil lease on his land, and he wasn't as broke these days as he was for a while. It didn't even have to be a clunker. He could buy something decent and sell it later. He'd feel like more of a man if he could pick up Kelly instead of having her drive them all the time.

He was thinking about calling J.J. to give him a ride to the lot when somebody rapped on the door. Probably one of the domino players needing a temporary partner. They often called on him if one of them had some work to do around the place.

Instead it was J.J. and a short, hefty guy wearing a suit.

"Hello, J.J. I was just about to call you."

"Guess I saved you the trouble. Cole, I'm sure you remember Mayor Fletcher."

Cole didn't, but he shook hands with the man and said, "Good to see you, Mayor. What can I do for you?"

The rattle of the dominoes in the outer office stopped, and J.J. said, "Can we come in and talk to you about something?"

"Sure." He stood aside for the men to enter, then closed the door. "What's up?"

"We've got a problem," the mayor said. "This morning Wally Gaskamp who owns the feed store was out walking with his dog and came across some bones down by the creek not far from here."

"Human?" Cole asked.

"Appear to be, but we're not sure," the mayor said. "We've got Ham Rayburn down guarding the site now."

"Who's Ham Rayburn?"

"Dick Rayburn's oldest boy. He signed on with the police force about six months ago."

"We need your help on this," J.J. said, and Cole felt a pump of adrenaline. "The police chief had a heart attack three days ago, and he's in Tyler having a bypass. The rest of the force are good boys, but they're kind of green, and this is out of my jurisdiction."

The mayor cleared his throat. "We thought, since you were in homicide and all, that you might step in as temporary chief and sort of a consultant. Just part-time, you understand, since you're recuperating. We'll make it worth your while."

"Be glad to help any way I can, but as long as I'm on medical leave from HPD I can't accept a formal position or compensation. I can act as a volunteer part-time—and be happy to oblige—but the problem is, I have a hard time getting around." He held up his cane.

"Oh, we can have one of the boys drive you," the mayor said.

"I can drive myself as soon as I get a car."

"Tell you what," the mayor said, "we'll loan you the chief's car. Almost new Mercury."

"Let me get my coat," Cole said.

Suddenly he felt alive again. Useful. Of course, he knew from experience that they might find anything from cow bones to an old cemetery corpse to a murder victim and anything in between, but still he was raring to go.

KELLY WAS FAMISHED by the time she arrived at the Twilight Tearoom to meet Cole for lunch. Lately she seemed to have the appetite of a horse, but she hadn't gained any weight, thank goodness.

Cole was already sitting at a table with J.J., and he waved when she entered. She felt a pang of guilt when she saw him; she still hadn't told him about the pregnancy. *Soon,* she told herself as she waved back. *Soon.*

Cole and J.J. rose as she approached.

"Good to see you, Dr. Kelly," J.J. said. "I was just leaving."

"Don't let me run you off."

"You're not. I have to get back to the office." To Cole he said, "See you later, Chief."

"Chief?" she asked.

A grin flashed from ear to ear. "You're looking at the new part-time, voluntary, temporary chief of police."

"Of where? Here?"

"Yep."

"That's wonderful. When did this happen?"

"Couple of hours ago," he said. He leaned forward and added quietly, "The town's in a bind, and I agreed to help out. I hate to have to cancel our plans for this afternoon, but we have a situation. Matter of fact, I could use your advice on something. Let's order, and I'll tell you about it."

She was eager to hear about what had put the new flash in his eyes and animation in his voice, so they ordered the Wednesday special and raspberry tea, and then he described what might be a crime scene in Naconiche.

"I've called in the Texas Rangers' crime lab unit, so I didn't want to disturb things too much until they arrive this afternoon, but the bones appear to be human. I've had a couple of graduate courses in forensic anthropology, not enough to make me an expert but enough to guess that this isn't some old burial ground that's come unearthed. Since we don't have a local medical examiner, I'd like your opinion.''

''It's definitely out of my field, but I'll help any way I can.''

AN HOUR AND A HALF LATER, Kelly and Cole stood on the creek bank where a cold, damp wind cut through the bare willow trees.

She turned up the collar on her coat. ''I agree,'' she said. ''Human. And, judging from that shoe you found, probably a woman, but not an elderly one, I would say, shorter than me but not by more than a couple of inches. I wouldn't begin to guess how long she's been here or how she died. Are you thinking murder?''

Cole shrugged. ''Too soon to tell. It could be an accident or natural causes. Do you know of anybody in town who's come up missing in the last couple of years?''

''Nobody comes to mind, but I'll think about it. Want me to ask around?''

''Not yet, but thanks. Let's wait until we have some more forensic information.'' He touched the tip of her nose, which she was sure rivaled Rudolph's. ''You're freezing out here. Let's get you back to your car.''

''What about you?''

''This comes with the new job. Could you give me a ride downtown to the station? It will be an hour at least before the Ranger unit arrives, and I have some things to do.''

"Sure," she said.

As they made their way up the uneven embankment, she noticed that it was a struggle for him, but she didn't comment or offer to help. Clearly he was excited by his new venture; she could sense the energy and focus it generated. He was like a kid at Christmas.

"Are you going to get a badge and a gun and a uniform and a key to the executive washroom?" she asked as they drove downtown.

"I'll get a car, and I already have a gun. I don't think I'll rate the chief's badge and uniform. I'll have to ask about the key."

"I think you'd look sexy in a uniform."

He grinned. "Think so?"

"Absolutely."

"I haven't worn a uniform in years. I'll have to see if I can scare one up for this weekend. I'll wear it, and you can wear that scanty little outfit you were telling me about—the one with the diamonds and the fishnet stockings you wore on stage."

"Are we going to a costume party?"

"Only to a very private one. In the bedroom."

"Planning something kinky?"

He chuckled and twirled an imaginary mustache. "I'll put some thought into it."

"No handcuffs."

"Right. Handcuffs are out." When she pulled up in front of the station, he said, "Sorry again about having to cancel our afternoon. How about dinner if I can shake away?"

"Sure. Give me a call." She watched him stride into the police station, his gait stronger than she had ever seen it. Some old bones by the creek were better medicine for him than anything in her drug cabinet.

The prospect of looking at used office furniture in Travis Lake didn't hold quite the allure that it had when Cole was going along. Hoping that Carrie might be in town, she called her apartment.

Carrie answered.

"You're back from Louisiana," Kelly said.

"Just got in town yesterday afternoon. What's up?"

"I have to make a trip to Travis Lake to look at a warehouse full of used office furniture this afternoon, and I thought you might like to ride over with me."

"Sure. I'd love to. I need to start furnishing my own office, and I may get some ideas. Why are you looking for office furniture?"

"For the hospice center."

"What time are we leaving?" Carrie asked.

"I'm in the car and about a minute from your place. No, make that a minute and a half. The light just changed."

"Let me put on some shoes, and I'll meet you downstairs in half a shake."

At about the time that Kelly pulled up in front of the fourplex that J. J. Outlaw owned, Carrie came out dressed in jeans and a sweater and pulling on a wind-breaker. Carrie had sold her town house in Houston and moved into the upstairs apartment J.J. vacated after he and Mary Beth married and moved into their new house. She spent a lot of time with Frank and the twins at his home, but for the sake of small town propriety and of the children, she maintained her own place.

"Brrrr," Carrie said as she hopped in the car. "It's colder than a brass bra in an Amarillo snowstorm."

Kelly laughed. "I've missed you, my friend. How are you?"

"Fine as frog fur. And back for good. I just finished the absolute very last project for my uncle's oil company. Between my being gone and your romance with my future brother-in-law, I don't think I've seen you but twice since Christmas, and that was at exercise class. I can't believe you're not with Cole this afternoon."

"He abandoned me for his new job."

"What new job?"

"He's sort of standing in part-time for the chief of police while our regular chief is out having heart surgery."

"Say, that's fantastic! Maybe he'll take the job permanently and you two can get married and we can be sisters-in-law."

Kelly only laughed. The chances of that happening were infinitesimal, but she had to confess that the same thought had flitted through her mind when Cole had told her about his new position. His staying and their getting married would solve a lot of problems.

She had long ago admitted to herself that she was in love with Cole, but he'd never said that he loved her, nor had he even hinted at a long-term commitment. That was one of the reasons she hadn't mentioned the baby. Like some naive teenager, a part of her hoped that Cole would discover that he was madly in love and couldn't live without her, decide to stay in Naconiche and propose so they could live happily ever after. Then she could spring the news of the baby. It wasn't likely to happen, but she didn't want a husband who married her only because he felt obligated. Such marriages rarely worked.

"You're awfully quiet," Carrie said.

"I was just thinking."

"About marrying Cole and being my sister-in-law?"

"Don't buy your bridesmaid dress yet. I believe he's been burned by marriage."

"That's what Frank says," Carrie told her. "I think he only married his ex-wife because she said she was pregnant."

A bolt of anxiety hit her, and she almost lost her breath. Trying to act casual, she said, "Really? I thought Cole didn't have children."

"He doesn't. Something happened. A miscarriage maybe. Frank didn't know. I gather Cole is pretty tight-lipped."

That bit of information complicated things enormously. She was filled with a heavy sense of foreboding. How was she going to tell Cole now? He was sure to feel that history was repeating itself. What was she going to do?

Plan on being a single mother—that's what she was going to do.

"You're awfully quiet," Carrie said. "Are you okay?"

Kelly desperately wanted to unburden herself to her friend, but because of the family connection, she didn't dare put Carrie in the position of having to keep a secret from Frank. She pasted on a big smile.

"I'm as fine as frog fur, to quote someone we know and love. When are you opening your new office?"

"In a couple of weeks. I'm going to share space with Dwight Murdock. He has an extra room in his suite that's only used for storage, and he'll be retiring soon so he wants me to begin taking over some of his practice. We'll share his secretary and the conference room. Think I can find a lawyerly desk and chair at this place we're going to?"

"I don't have a clue. Florence Russo scouted the place and gave me a list of items to check out. If I approve, I'll buy them and have them delivered to the hospice center. She said that the prices were great, and we have a limited budget."

"How about I donate a desk or something?" Carrie said.

"I wouldn't turn down the offer. And it's tax deductible, you know."

"Even better. Maybe I'll donate two. How's the hospice project coming?"

"Better than I had hoped. We're going to start interviews for a director in about ten days. That's why we're trying desperately to get the center fixed up by then. Having Florence on the committee was a godsend. Thanks for recommending her."

"Thank Mary Beth. She's the one who told me how helpful Florence was in restoring the tearoom and the inn."

The warehouse was just down from the old railroad station in Travis Lake. No passenger trains stopped there anymore, but the town had converted the gold and brown depot into a museum with a coffee bar.

"How neat," Carrie said as they passed the depot.

"You've never been there? We'll stop by later, and I'll buy you a latte."

"Sounds good. I'm a cheap date."

The warehouse was huge. And dusty. But there were some great bargains under the dust. A pimply faced kid with his cap backward showed them around and pointed out the items that Florence had tagged. Kelly bought everything plus a lateral file for her own office that she spotted.

Carrie found a great desk, credenza and bookcases as well as a super comfortable leather chair and a pair of client chairs. She also bought a lateral file identical to Kelly's.

"I'm fixed up," Carrie said after they paid for the purchases and made arrangements for delivery. "I can't believe my luck. I bought everything I'll need in less than an hour at less than half the price I was expecting to pay. A couple of pictures and a potted plant, and I'll be ready for business. Remind me to send flowers to Florence. She's a gem."

"I know. Dixie adores her."

"Of course she does," Carrie said as they left the warehouse. "Florence also baby-sits. Six kids. Or is it seven? Can you imagine?"

"Dixie and Jack seem to manage fine. Do you and Frank plan to have any more?"

"You know, we have talked about it. I never thought I was cut out to be a mommy, but I adore the twins, and I wouldn't mind having another. That old biological clock thing I suppose. And speaking of biological clocks, you and the new chief better step things up if you intend to have a family. You're older than I am."

Kelly wanted to blurt out her news, but she held off. "Thanks for reminding that I'm getting long in the tooth."

Carrie laughed. "We're not getting old, sweetie. We're in our prime. Want to do our number again for the Fall Follies this year?"

"I'm not sure Warren Iverson's heart can take it." *Or that I'll be able to fit into that scanty outfit.*

Carrie started singing "Diamonds Are a Girl's Best Friend," and Kelly joined in. By the time they reached the depot, they were harmonizing at the top of their lungs.

KELLY WAS STILL HUMMING when she went in her back door. She and Carrie had had a great time. They had sung show tunes all the way home. Carrie had decided that they would perform a number from *Chicago* for this year's follies. Kelly couldn't tell her that she'd be a new mother by then and in no shape to be prancing around a stage in scanty attire—even if she gave a flip about Warren Iverson's heart.

No cats met her as she went in. They were probably upstairs with Gladys. The disloyal scamps spent more time in the garage apartment with the maid than they did with her. She had resorted to thick socks to keep her feet warm in bed—on the nights that Cole didn't provide the service.

She called Florence and related the results of her excursion to the warehouse. "They'll deliver everything Friday afternoon between three and five. Can you be there?"

"No problem," Florence said. "Would you let

Gladys know? She promised to give the place a good cleaning before the furniture arrives.''

"I'll do that. Bye.''

Kelly grabbed an apple to munch on while she checked the mail, then headed out to talk to Gladys.

As she neared the top of the apartment steps, she could see Gladys through the window. The TV was on, Gladys was in the recliner sound asleep and both cats were curled up in her lap. They all looked so content that she didn't have the heart to disturb them, so she turned and tiptoed down the stairs.

The phone was ringing when she opened the back door.

It was Cole.

"Sorry, darlin', but I'm going to have to take a rain check on dinner. I've got a bunch of things hanging loose here, and I need to work late. How about tomorrow night?''

"Can't. It's Thursday. Exercise class and hospital rounds.''

"Oh, right,'' he said, sounding distracted. "Hang on.'' She could hear muffled conversation. "Friday better?''

"If I don't have an emergency.''

"Fine. I'll talk to you later.'' He hung up.

"Fine?'' She glared at the phone. *Fine?* She slammed down the receiver and plopped on the couch, thoroughly ticked.

Everybody had deserted her.

Only one thing to do. Make a double batch of chocolate chip cookies with pecans.

And she didn't intend to give Cole Outlaw a single one.

Chapter Thirteen

When Cole called to beg off Friday dinner, too, Kelly was so dejected that she decided to make brownies. "Don't brownies sound good, boys?" she asked the cats, who'd deigned to spend the evening with her since Gladys had gone for a weekend visit with her niece in San Augustine.

She'd just gotten out her mixing bowl when the phone rang again. It was Matt McKee, one of her oldest and dearest friends. A year older than she was, he'd lived two doors down from her when they were growing up, and they had played together from the time they were preschoolers. She adored Matt, and even though their paths diverged from time to time, their friendship had endured for a lot of years. They had shared secrets and fought battles with each other and for each other; he'd taken her to the prom when she was humiliated that she didn't have a date, and she'd done similar things for him.

"Matt, it's great to hear from you! I thought you'd fallen off the earth. It's been ages."

"I know it, sugar plum, and I need a Kelly fix. You doing anything exciting tonight?"

"You mean besides watching my toenails grow?"

He laughed. "Sounds like you need some company. I'm on my way back to Dallas from a convention in Shreveport, and I thought I might take a little jog down your way if you're not busy."

"I'd love to see you. Is Jeff with you?"

"No, he's in Dublin on business. Can I bunk on your couch tonight?"

"My couch isn't long enough for you, but I have a guest room."

"Sounds great. Get your glad rags on, and I'll take you to the finest restaurant in that one-horse town."

"The finest restaurant here doesn't serve dinner, and the second best is the Burger Barn."

"I have a sudden hankering for a double meat cheeseburger with bacon and fries. I'll be there in half an hour or so."

Kelly put away the mixing bowl and freshened her makeup. The prospect of seeing Matt had her humming again.

COLE WAS SITTING at the chief's desk going through a pile of paperwork when the phone rang.

"Hey, Chief, it's Ham Rayburn."

"I'm not the chief," he told the young cop. "I'm only a consultant."

"Okay, Chief. Listen, my girlfriend and I are at the Burger Barn, and Emma Ann thought you ought to know that Dr. Martin is here with some tall, good-looking dude."

"Who?"

"Dunno. Not anybody from around here. Want me to check his ID?"

"What's he doing?"

"Right now he's eating an onion ring," Ham reported.

"Unless he's breaking any laws, I think you should skip the ID check."

"Ten-four."

Cole had barely hung up the phone when J.J. strolled in. "Hey, big brother, what are you doing here at this time of night?"

"Trying to locate all the missing person reports for the area. I don't think anything has been filed in this place since 1986."

"Hey, you only signed on as a part-time consultant," J.J. said, "not a one-man department. Somebody's moving in on your girl while you're holed up here shuffling papers."

"What are you talking about?"

"We just came from the Burger Barn, and—"

"Who's *we?*"

"Mary Beth and Katy and me. They're waiting in the truck. Anyhow, I figured that you ought to know that Dr. Kelly is out carousing with what Mary Beth called the most gorgeous hunk of man she'd ever seen in her life. I would've gone over and punched his lights out on general principles, 'cept he's bigger than me. I don't know who he is, but he looked sort of familiar. Mary Beth thought he might be a movie star or something."

Cole felt his blood beginning to simmer, but he kept a calm bearing, shrugging. "Last I heard, it's a free country. She can go out with anybody she wants to."

"No skin off my nose," J.J. said, "but if it was

me, I'll be pissed enough to hustle my tail over to the Burger Barn.''

"But it's *not* you, little brother. And instead of going to the Burger Barn, I need to get back to the inn. Dad's minding the office until I get home.''

"By the way, I've been meaning to tell you that one of the downstairs tenants in my fourplex is moving out this week. You interested in moving in?''

"I might be. Is Mary Beth firing me?''

"Naw. If you want to stay on in the manager's apartment and pull night duty, it's fine with her, but we just figured that you might want a little more freedom now that you're getting around better.'' J.J. shot him a possum-eating grin and added, "Course if Dr. Kelly is taking up with somebody else, you might not need any more freedom at night.''

"Why don't you get out of here and quit making your wife and daughter sit out in the truck in the cold while you tend to my business.''

"The engine's running and the heater's on. Besides, who do you think insisted we come here?''

By the time J.J. finally ambled out, Cole felt like he was straddling an electric fence. He grabbed the phone and called the Twilight Inn. When his father answered he said, "Pop, how about you turn on the No Vacancy sign, forward phone calls to my cell and go on home. I'm going to stop and get a bite to eat.''

"You're welcome to come by and eat with us,'' his dad said.

"No, I think I'm in the mood for a hamburger.''

"Funny you should mention that. You've had a couple of calls suggesting that you might want to go by the Burger Barn. I hear Dr. Kelly is sharing a table with a tall, good-looking stranger.''

Cole didn't say anything for two beats, then asked, ''Who called?''

''Reba Conroy and your brother.''

''J.J.?''

''No, Frank.''

''Who the devil is Reba Conroy?''

''Friend of your mama's and one of the biggest meddlers in town. And, son, far be it from me to interfere in your business, but maybe you ought to avoid the Burger Barn tonight.''

''Why?''

This time it was his father who hesitated a couple of beats. ''I'll turn on the sign and forward the calls. Good night, son.''

Cole tried to tell himself that there was a perfectly legitimate reason for Kelly to be having dinner with some guy. He was probably a doctor from Travis Lake or something. Or maybe a drug salesman. Or even a prospective donor to the hospice program. There could be a dozen explanations.

And in any case, he had no strings on her.

He kept telling himself that, but by the time he locked up and got in the car, he was in a horn-tossing mood. Stomping on the accelerator and cursing under his breath, he roared off toward the Burger Barn.

Just as he pulled into the parking lot, he spotted Kelly and the guy coming out the front door. In the dim light he couldn't tell much about the man except that he was tall, broad-shouldered and blond. They were laughing and had their arms around each other's waists.

Son of a bitch! Cole could feel steam coming out of every joint.

Seething, he watched as the bastard helped Kelly into a sports car that cost more than he made in a year. They were so wrapped up in each other that they hadn't seen him. He slunk down in his seat and waited until they pulled away.

Then he pulled out behind them.

They drove directly to Kelly's house. When they turned into the driveway, he cut his lights and coasted to a stop across the street. Something must have been damned funny because they were still laughing when they crawled out of the car.

Cole ground his molars.

When the guy popped the trunk and took out a garment bag, he could have chewed nails.

"Son of a bitch!" he muttered. He wanted to go rip that bag out of the guy's hands and strangle him with it.

He sat there and seethed for a couple of minutes after they went inside, trying to get hold of himself. There went the theory that he was a drug salesman. Or…maybe he was. Some job.

Well, if she wanted to get it on with a traveling salesman while his back was turned, more power to her. Like he told J.J., they didn't have any kind of understanding. Of course, he never figured her for the kind to sleep around with every man who came along, either. If he wasn't enough to satisfy the good doctor, to hell with her.

He pulled away, telling himself that it didn't matter that Kelly was entertaining an overnight guest. Her business, not his. He'd go home and watch a rerun of that New York cop show. Yep. That's what he'd do. Nuke some supper and watch TV.

The devil he would!

Halfway back to the motel, he wheeled into a convenience store. Kelly Martin was his, dammit! And he wasn't slinking off like a dog with his tail between his legs. A resurgence of anger put a fire in his belly, and he hurried inside the store.

"Got any antihistamines?" he asked the kid behind the counter.

"A bunch. What kind you want?"

"The strongest ones you got."

While the kid picked out a box from the shelf behind him, Cole grabbed a package of little powdered donuts and a cup of coffee. After he paid for the items, he popped four pills from the blister pack and washed them down with coffee.

Tasted worse than roofing tar, and he dumped the cup. He should've remembered that the coffee here was awful. He stuffed the rest of the pills in his pocket and unwrapped the donuts when he got to the car. He wasn't hungry, but he figured he needed something to sop up the acid in his gut before it ate a hole and started leaking.

He'd polished off the whole package of donuts by the time he got back to Kelly's, and that didn't take long. Still steamed, he'd tried to talk himself down. No need to go in with guns blazing. He was going to do his damnedest to play it cool. Or croak trying.

His knock on Kelly's back door was louder than he'd meant it to be. It rang out like a shotgun blast in the quiet neighborhood.

He waited.

And waited.

Finally the door opened and a big guy who had at least two inches on him stood there with a cat on his shoulder and another one twining around his legs. The bastard grinned and flashed dimples deep enough to mine coal. "Yes?"

Mary Beth was right. With his wavy blond hair and blue silk shirt, he looked like somebody from the movies—and vaguely familiar.

"Is Kelly here?" What a dumb thing to say. Of course she was here.

"And you are…?"

"I'm a cop," Cole growled.

"Who is it?" Kelly shouted from a distance.

"He says he's a cop," the guy called over the shoulder without the cat on it. "Haven't you been paying your parking tickets?"

"I'm not that kind of cop."

"Oh, hi, Cole," Kelly said as she came to the door. "This is Dr. Matt McKee, one of my oldest friends from Dallas."

"Oldest and *dearest,* darlin'," Matt said crushing her to his side with both arms and dropping a kiss on her forehead. "Don't forget the dearest."

"Cut it out, Matt." Kelly laughed and swatted pretty boy on the butt.

"I'm her newest *dearest* friend," Cole ground out.

Matt's eyebrows went up, and he looked amused.

"Matt, this is Cole Outlaw. He's the new temporary, part-time, volunteer consultant and acting police chief of Naconiche."

"Oh, that kind of cop," Matt said, offering his hand. "Sounds like an interesting job."

Cole wanted to rip the bastard's tongue out and beat his pretty face bloody. Instead he switched his cane and shook hands with a firm grip. "What kind of a doctor are you?" he asked, scowling at the smug-looking cat. "A vet?"

"Nope. Just finished my residency in ophthalmology. I got a late start."

Kelly looked at Cole and made a brushing motion beside her mouth. "I was about to make coffee. We'd invite you in, but as you see, the cats have latched on to Matt and won't let go." She made another brushing motion at the corner of her mouth. "Cole is allergic to cats," she explained to Matt.

"That must be tough," Matt said. "I love cats."

"No problem," Cole said. "I took some antihistamine, and I'd love a good cup of coffee." He whacked Matt with his cane as he bulled his way inside. "Sorry," he mumbled. But he wasn't a bit sorry. He wanted to do worse.

He gimped his way into the kitchen after Kelly while her company swaggered along with his cat stole.

The silence hung heavy as Kelly measured coffee for the pot. And it appeared to him that she was dumping the grounds a little more vigorously than she usually did. Matt simply leaned against the island looking as if he were posing for the cover of *Cat Fancier Magazine.*

"You and Kelly have been friends for a long time, you say?" he asked Matt.

"About thirty years. I gave Kelly her first kiss." He flashed his dimples.

Cole wanted to slug him. "That so?" he managed to grind out.

Kelly ripped off a paper towel so hard that the roll came loose from the holder, bounced and unwound across the floor.

"I'll get it, darlin'," Matt said, bounding to the rescue.

While Mr. *GQ* was helping, Kelly strode to Cole and thrust the wad in her hand to him. She looked a little miffed. Too bad. If anyone had a right to be miffed it was him. He wasn't leaving so she could shack up with Romeo.

He looked down at the paper towel. "What's this for?"

"You have powder on the sides of your mouth."

He felt like a damned fool. "Must have been that donut."

"No doubt. I thought you were working late tonight."

"I was. I did. I was trying to check missing person reports."

"Cole was a homicide detective in Houston," Kelly said as she led the three of them into the den. "And he's helping with an incident we've had in town. Someone found human remains by a creek bank here a couple of days ago."

"Interesting," Matt said as he and Kelly and the cats sat on the sofa.

Cole took an easy chair across from them. "Foul play?"

"Don't know yet," Cole said. "The DPS lab in Austin has a team of forensic experts doing an autopsy. We should have more information next week."

Looking at Matt, he kept getting the feeling that he knew him from somewhere. *Matt. Matt McKee. That had a familiar—* "Matt McKee. It just dawned on me. Didn't you play quarterback for the Packers?"

Matt laughed. "Ruined my knee and froze my ass off on the bench for two years. I was glad to get back to Texas."

"I remember when you got hurt. A real shame. I also remember when you played at UT. Never will forget that game with the Aggies when you threw five touchdown passes. What was that receiver's name— the little guy that ran like greased lightning?"

"Boles. Elijah Boles."

"I'll get the coffee," Kelly said.

"What ever happened to him?" Cole asked.

"He owns a movie theater and sells real estate in Tyler. I hear from him every once in a while. Too bad he didn't get drafted for the pros. His hands were made of Super Glue, and he could outrun anybody I've ever seen."

Kelly served the coffee while he and Matt talked football, then she said, "I'm going to make some brownies," and left.

One of the cats came sniffing around him, and Cole discreetly toed him away, then asked Matt, "How do you feel about the Cowboys' new tight end?"

"I think he has some real potential when he gets a little more experience. It was a good trade."

A couple of times he felt himself nodding off while they were talking, but he shook off his sleepiness. He wasn't leaving if he had to prop his eyes open with toothpicks.

"Cole! Cole!" Kelly said. "Your cell phone is ringing."

"Huh?" He rubbed his face and grabbed the phone. "Hello."

"I need some ice," a male voice boomed.

"What do you want me to do about it?"

"Bring it to me."

"I don't have any ice. You're on your own, buddy." He tossed the phone aside.

"Who was that?" Kelly asked.

"Beats me. I thought you were going to bake some brownies."

"I already did. There's a plate of them on the coffee table."

He stretched his eyes wide and rubbed his face again. "They look good."

"Cole, what kind of antihistamines did you take?"

"These." He fished the blister pack from his pocket and tossed it to her. He missed.

Good old Matt retrieved it for her.

"How many did you take?"

"Whatever's gone. I bought them on my way here."

"Good Lord!" she said. "No wonder you keeping slurring your words and falling asleep. You've OD'd on allergy pills."

Both Kelly and Matt got up. Kelly stretched his lids open and peered into his eyes while Matt took his pulse.

"What do you think?" Kelly asked.

"I think he'll live," Matt said.

"Of course I'll live. I told you that I'm fine."

"You're not fine," Kelly said. "You took twice the normal dosage of antihistamine."

"It seems to have worked. I haven't sneezed once."

Kelly gave a snort and glanced heavenward. "Like you would know. The kind you took tends to make many people drowsy, and I'd say that you're one of them. You're loopy. I'd send you home, but you don't need to be driving. You'd wrap yourself around a tree or something."

"No, I'm fine. Really. Not a bit sleepy. You follow baseball, Matt?"

Matt chuckled. "I think we covered that already."

"You've covered everything but water polo and curling," Kelly said, rising. "The testosterone in this room is getting too strong for me. I'm going to bed."

He started to say, "I'll go with you," but he couldn't quit get the words out.

Chapter Fourteen

Cole woke up to the smell of bacon and with a crick in his neck. He raised up and looked around. He was lying on Kelly's couch with a blanket thrown over him. Raking his fingers through his hair, then holding his head, he tried to remember the night before.

"Well, good morning," a deep voice said. "About time you came around."

He peered through swollen eyelids. Matt McKee.

It all came back.

Well, most of it.

"What time is it?"

"Eight-seventeen. How do you like your eggs?"

"Scrambled. Where's Kelly?"

"In the shower. And the cats are upstairs in the garage apartment."

"You spent the night here?"

"I did." An hour seemed to pass before Matt added, "In the guest room. You like grape jelly or strawberry preserves?"

Cole let go of the breath he was holding. He was in no shape to take on McKee this morning, and he would have had to try if he'd slept with Kelly. "Anything's fine but orange marmalade."

"I don't know anybody who eats the stuff except my aunt Rose. I take all my little jars of it home from hotels for her. I think the manufacturers must pay the hotels to take it off their hands."

"No doubt. Did I make a fool of myself last night?"

Matt laughed. "Not too bad. The man in Unit 6 called on your cell phone again wanting some ice."

"Unit 6?" He groaned. "Oh, God. What did I say to him?"

"I took the second call and ran a bag of ice over to him. He'd twisted his ankle and needed it for the swelling. I wrapped it for him while I was there."

"Thanks for taking care of that. I don't know what happened to me. I feel like I've been dragged through a knothole backward."

"You took an overdose of antihistamines and have a hangover. Stick with the prescription ones if you're going to hang around the cats. You're in love with our girl, aren't you?"

"Kelly? I've only known her for a few weeks."

"Sometimes it doesn't take long," Matt said. "She's a wonderful person. She deserves someone who will cherish her and make her world complete. If you hurt her, I'll break both your legs."

Cole looked up at him. There was nothing pretty about Matt then. His expression was fierce. "You love her yourself."

"Of course. I adore her. Always have. But you don't have to sweat any competition from me if that's on your mind. I'm gay," Matt said, then laughed uproariously.

Cole hung his head in his hands. Now he really did feel like a damned fool. What had happened to his good sense? He was usually Mr. Supercool. He didn't go off half-cocked. He had to get out of there before he had to face Kelly.

Struggling to his feet, he said, "I've gotta get home. Matt, it was good to meet you. Tell Kelly to give me a call later."

"Don't run off yet. The biscuits are almost done."

"Thanks, but I can't stay. I've got an appointment."

Cursing himself for a blamed idiot, he hightailed it out of there and headed for the motel. God, what a fiasco. He'd gone charging in to save Kelly from the clutches of a guy who was more likely to put a move on him than on her. What was worse was that—gay or not—he'd really liked Matt.

His indignant lover bit had tanked. Kelly was bound to be pissed at him, and he couldn't blame her.

Howard was manning the desk when he arrived. "Mornin'," the old man said. "Looks like you had a rough night. You must have heard about Dr. Kelly."

Cole scowled. "What about her?"

"Word around town is that she was down at the Burger Barn last night with a tall, handsome gent. I didn't see 'em myself, you understand, but Curtis's youngest daughter did. Some said he was a movie star. Others thought he might be one of those models that pose on romance books. Oscar Hunnicutt said he was a big-time football player. Folks around here don't know what to make of it. They thought you and her were a couple.''

"Folks around here tend to stick their noses into other people's business too much.''

Howard gave a little cackle. "I'll grant you that. Are you and Dr. Kelly on the outs?''

"Nope.'' He went into his apartment and slammed the door.

He'd been gone from Naconiche too long. He'd forgotten how everybody knew everybody else's business. And how old-fashioned most of the people were. With all the time he and Kelly had spent together, the town probably had them madly in love and engaged by now.

They were a long way from engaged. Sure, he cared about her. His reaction to Matt last night had proved that. He'd been jealous. Worse than jealous. So he had to care about her. But love? He wasn't even sure he knew what love was.

He had to do some thinking.

But first he needed a shower and a cup of coffee.

MATT TOSSED HIS BAG in the trunk, then hugged Kelly. "You take care of yourself, sugar plum. And if that baby ends up needing a daddy, I'll marry you.''

Kelly smiled. "I'm sure Jeff would be thrilled about that.''

"He'd probably offer to marry you himself. But I don't think you have any reason to be concerned. It's obvious that Cole's crazy about you. I liked him, by the way.''

"How could you tell? He was zonked.''

"He's a good man. I think you ought to let him

know right away that you're pregnant. He has a right to make his own decision."

"Soon," she said. "Thanks for listening to my troubles, and thanks for your generous donation to our hospice program. It will pay staffing costs for a year."

"If you need more, let me know. And if you need a shoulder, let me know that, too."

"You're a dear, dear friend, Matt KcKee," she said, giving him a last hug. "Drive carefully."

She waved to Matt until he'd driven out of sight, then went upstairs to the apartment to check on the cats.

They had plenty of food and water and showed no interest in going home with her. They were either miffed about being ousted last night, or they had found a new home. Cole would be happy if it were the latter.

Cole. She had to call him. And sooner or later she had to tell him about the baby.

Later, she decided. She wasn't ready yet.

When she went downstairs and telephoned him, he answered on the first ring. "How are you feeling this morning?" she asked.

"Sheepish. Are you ready to fry my liver?"

"Hannibal Lecter I'm not. Are you working to-day?"

"Nope. Not much I can do until Monday. Are you on call this weekend?"

"Nope," she said. "I'm free as a bird."

"I need to make a trip to Houston to pick up some of my things from the apartment and get my car. I hate for it to sit up too long without being driven.

You interested in going with me and staying overnight?''

''Sure. What do I need to pack?''

''Your toothbrush. And maybe that sexy song-and-dance outfit you told me about.''

She laughed. ''No, I meant for dinner or something.''

''Nothing fancy. There are some great ethnic restaurants in my neighborhood—Indian, Thai, Chinese, Mexican, Italian. You can take your pick.''

''I pick Thai. I'll be by in about an hour.''

She made it in fifty-five minutes.

''Good to see you around here, Dr. Kelly,'' Howard said as she came into the office.

''Thank you.'' She knocked on the door to Cole's unit.

''We were all a mite worried about that new feller you were sharing a hamburger with last night. Which is he—a model, a movie star or a football player?''

She fought a laugh. ''Matt is a doctor, an ophthalmologist and an old friend, but he used to play football.''

''I swan,'' Howard said. ''Oscar was right.''

''Right about what?'' Cole asked.

''Never you mind,'' Howard said. ''You leaving?''

''Yep.''

She could tell that Howard was itching to know the particulars, but after Cole's curt answer, he only said, ''Have a nice day.''

On the way to her car Kelly asked, ''Who's handling the night shift while you're gone?''

''A college kid that Mary Beth is trying out for full-time employment. I'm moving into one of J.J.'s apartments next week. Living at the inn was great for a while, but it's like living in a blasted fishbowl. I'm looking forward to having some privacy.'' Once they'd pulled out of the parking lot, Cole said, "I wouldn't be surprised if half the people in town weren't watching us out their windows with binoculars."

"More than half, I'd estimate. That's one of the few drawbacks to living in a small town. There aren't many secrets. I can't tell you how many calls I've had this morning wanting to know about the man I had dinner with and about the cars parked in my driveway all night."

"They should get a life. Kelly, I'm sorry I acted like such a jerk off last night. I—"

"No need to apologize. To tell the truth I was a little flattered."

"Flattered?"

"Sure." She smiled. "You were jealous of Matt."

"Jealous? Me?"

"Yes, you."

He chuckled. "Yeah, I guess I'll have to admit I was. Funny, I'm usually not the jealous type." He rested his hand on her shoulder and stroked the side of her neck with his thumb. "I care a lot about you, and I didn't take to the notion of somebody moving in on you."

He *cared a lot*. Well, that was a step in the right direction, she thought. Should she push? No. Wait.

KELLY FELT HERSELF tensing as they passed through Humble at the outer edges of the city. Although the freeway lanes doubled, the traffic grew heavier, and she spotted a jet climbing across their route from the airport to their right. The smells changed. Even inside the car she got a whiff of chemical plants and exhaust fumes. People who lived there rarely noticed. They were used to it, but she'd become accustomed to clean air and a slower pace. Even though she'd grown up in Dallas and was no stranger to hustle and bustle, the city made her jumpy now. She had to admit that the shopping was great, and Houston had some of the best restaurants and entertainment opportunities in the country, but the thought of having to live in this mess gave her the willies.

His apartment complex was on the west side just inside the loop and not too far from the Galleria, the upscale shopping center that was bumper to bumper all the time.

She pulled into a parking space that he indicated and popped open the trunk to get her things. Cole reached for her bag, but she said, "I'll handle it. You're going to have to navigate three flights of stairs."

"This may be the ultimate test of my physical therapy sessions."

"Just take it slow," she said.

He didn't set any speed records—and he looked as if he wanted to trip a young hard-body that bounded past them taking the steps two at a time—but with a couple of rest stops, he made it.

"I can't believe that I purposely picked the third floor to help me keep in shape," Cole said when he reached the top. "If I had to stay here now, I'd become a hermit. I need to check with the office and ask about moving to a ground-floor unit."

Her heart lurched when he spoke of moving back to Houston as if it were a given. His comment shouldn't have surprised her; he'd never acted eager to stay in Naconiche. She stood there with a lump in her throat while he unlocked the door and turned on a light. When she could swallow the lump down, she said, "Are you planning on moving back here soon?"

"Depends on what the doctor here says in a few weeks. If he thinks I'm able to go back to work, that's what I'll do. They'll probably stick me on a desk job until I can retire."

"When can you retire?"

"I'll have my twenty in two years from this June."

Kelly dropped her bag inside the door and took off her jacket. "What about taking medical disability? Two years can seem like forever if you're doing something you don't like."

"Don't I know it. I haven't got a clue what I'm going to do, but I've got to make a living somehow, and I don't want to blow my pension. It's a little musty in here," he said, "but not too bad. The cleaning people have been coming by to check on things and keep the place up." He crossed the room to open the balcony door and let in some fresh air.

"Nice," she said as she wandered around the combination living-dining room, which had a small kitchen to one side, separated by a tiled bar.

And it was nice—in a Spartan kind of way. A brown leather couch faced a small fireplace along with a heavy rustic coffee table, which held only a remote control and a neat stack of magazines. A floor lamp sat at one end of the couch and a TV tray at the other. The only other piece of furniture in the living room was a big TV and entertainment system in an open cabinet. No pictures hung on the white walls. There were no plants, no accessories of any kind except for two tapestry pillows and a dark green throw on the couch, which she suspected were more utilitarian than decorative. But the bookshelves on each side of the fireplace were crammed full of books.

Instead of a table in the dining area, there was a desk with a state-of-the-art computer and printer, a filing cabinet and two more bookshelves filled with books.

"Pretty awful, isn't it?" Cole asked.

"Not at all. It looks like a bachelor's apartment." She strolled to the bookshelves by the fireplace and ran her fingers along the spines, examining the titles. There were several novels, but most of the books were academic looking—criminal justice, psychology, sociology, forensic science.

"I'm not much on doodads."

"I noticed." She smiled. "But you're big on books. Have you read all these?"

"Yep."

She drew out one on forensic hypnosis and flipped through the pages. "Impressive."

He took the book from her, laid it on the mantel and pulled her into his arms. "Just because I'm a cop doesn't mean that I'm dumb."

She rested her arms on his shoulders, crossing them behind his neck. "I never for one minute thought you were dumb." She rubbed his nose with hers. "Stubborn, yes. Macho, yes. Dumb…no."

"You think I'm stubborn?"

"As a mule."

He grinned. "And macho?"

"Very." She pulled his mouth toward hers. "Macho turns me on."

His kiss was warm and hungry and thrilled her in that special way that his kisses always did. She wanted to meld her skin and his, feel his heart beating in her chest, and she pulled him closer, reveling in his touch, his strength, his scent. Even the taste of him excited her. She loved everything about Cole Outlaw. Everything.

"Mmmm, you feel good," he murmured against her mouth as his hands stroked her bottom and ground her against him. "What is it about you that gets under my skin and makes me do crazy things?"

"I don't know. You tell me." She gave a little gasp when his hand slipped under her sweater to stroke her breast.

"I like *that*," he said. "I'm a sucker for a D cup."

"I'm game."

He chuckled. "Want to see my bedroom?"

"Do you have mirrors on the ceiling?"

"No, but I can tape up some aluminum foil if that will get your motor running."

"My motor is already running."

Chapter Fifteen

Snuggled comfortably in Cole's arms, Kelly said, "I think the mirrors would have been redundant."

"Definitely."

"Want to stay here and order in pizza?"

"Nope. I'm going to treat you to some of the best Thai food you've ever eaten."

"Sure you feel like tackling those stairs twice?"

"Yep. But I'm going to take a load of stuff down to the car when we go so that I won't have to make an extra trip."

"What kind of stuff?"

"Clothes and my laptop. Some books. Mind helping?"

"Not at all. You want the bathroom first?"

They decided that he would grab a quick shower so that she could take her time dressing while he gathered the belongings he wanted to carry back to Naconiche. When he came out of the bathroom with a blue towel draped over his hips, he looked so sexy that she jerked the wrap away and rubbed herself against him.

"Sure you don't want to stay here and order pizza?" she asked coyly.

Laughing, he snatched the towel and popped her bottom with it. "Get away from me, Jezebel. I've got a yen for Panang, and I've already made reservations."

"Is the place that fancy?"

"No. That popular. But the owner and I go way back. Prepare to be pampered and stuffed."

By the time she'd dressed in dark wool slacks and a moss-green sweater, Cole had finished packing and had laid out a full garment bag on the bed. He looked absolutely sinful in all black—black sweater, black slacks, black boots. She wrapped her arms around him from the back and pressed her cheek against his shoulder blade.

He was so dear to her. She wanted desperately to tell him that she loved him.

Instead she broke away. "Ready?"

"Yes. Think you can handle this?" He picked up the garment bag.

"No problem. Let me get my coat."

When they started out of the apartment, Cole hefted a duffel bag by the door.

"Let me carry that, too," she said. "You need to use your cane and the handrail to be safe."

"It's heavy."

"Do I look like a lightweight?" She took the duffel from him, and it almost jerked her arm from its socket. "Good Lord! What do you have in here?"

"Mostly books. Can you manage it?"

"Of course." She charged out the door. "What in the world are you going to do with so many books?"

"Research."

"I just love the way you gush about your activities."

"Boring research."

"*Ohhh!* That explains everything." She rolled her eyes. "How do you know that I'd be bored?"

"I just never figured you for the type who'd be interested in urban homicide statistics."

"You're right. Statistics was my least favorite course in college."

On the way down the stairs, she was glad to stop and rest on the landings. She was convinced that her right arm would be two inches longer than her left when they got to the bottom.

They stowed the stuff in the trunk of her car, but they took Cole's SUV to the restaurant, which was only a few blocks away, off Westheimer. The Dancing Cat was tucked among one- and two-story shops in a center that was old enough to give it some character. Gnarled live oaks festooned with tiny white lights spread their branches over the walkways and people shopping or dining at one of the several interesting looking spots.

The parking lot was full, but they lucked out when a couple slid into a red car two doors down from the restaurant. Cole wheeled into the space, and they got out in front of a quaint store that sold clocks and watches. As they passed the flower shop next door, she stopped to admire several moss-covered pots of orchids in the glass display case and to sniff a profusion of daffodils blooming in the window box.

"Just smell these," she said, tugging at his hand. "They're heavenly."

"They make me sneeze."

She sighed. "A pity."

"Yeah, it is," he drawled as he laced his fingers with hers. "Let's eat. I'm starving."

"You're always starving."

He grinned. "For one thing or another."

"I assume you've been to an allergist."

"My appetites are out of their bailiwick." He held open the red door of the restaurant for her to enter.

"Don't be obtuse, Cole Younger Outlaw. If you haven't been to an allergist in a while, you should make an appointment and go in. There have been some marvelous new advances in the field."

"Yes, ma'am. I'll do that. Which allergist in Naconiche would you recommend?"

"Well...there isn't one."

He tapped the end of her nose. "Then I guess I'll have to wait a while on that, Dr. Martin."

About a dozen people were sitting or milling around in the cozy waiting area, and a small, serene-looking man was at a stand just beyond. The man's face lit up with a bright smile when he spotted them, and he hurried over.

"Ah, Cole, it's so good to see you!"

"Hello, Kusa. It's good to see you, too."

"Your table is ready. Follow me. Follow me."

When they were seated in an alcove of the small, beautifully decorated dining room, Cole introduced Kelly to Kusa, a Thai of middle age who was the owner.

"Welcome to The Dancing Cat," Kusa said to Kelly. As he handed them large menus, he added, "I was worried about this one and eager to hear from him. It's good to see my old friend walking about, even with a cane. What will you have to drink?"

"Your special tea," Cole said.

"I will send Sanun with it immediately," Kusa said, "along with appetizers I choose myself. Anything you want, you have only to ask." He bowed slightly and left.

"A nice man," Kelly said. "He's obviously very fond of you."

"I've known him for ten or twelve years. I met him when this place was robbed and his younger brother killed."

"How terrible. Did you find who did it?"

"Damned right. And recovered most of the money. Kusa and his family were very grateful. They would feed me every day for free if I'd let them. They have a hard time understanding HPD rules." He opened his menu. "What's your favorite?"

"Oh, I love that chicken soup with coconut milk and herbs. What's it called?"

"Tom Kha Khai. They make the best in town here."

Sanun, who turned out to be Kusa's oldest son, arrived with tea and a huge platter of assorted appetizers while they studied the menus. She settled on the soup and a shrimp and squid dish while Cole stuck with Panang, the beef curry he'd had a yen for, and the same chicken soup she'd ordered.

"These spring rolls are to die for," she said, reaching for a second. "I haven't had Thai food in ages, and I used to eat it all the time when I was doing my internship and residency here."

"Where did you live in Houston?"

"In an apartment by the Astrodome, near the medical center."

"What street?"

When she named the street and the complex she'd lived in, he chuckled. "I know the area well. I used to live there."

"You're kidding. When?"

When they compared notes, they discovered that he'd lived in the next building during the first two years of her internship.

"Small world after all," she said. "A pity we didn't meet then."

"You might have saved me from a very bad marriage. But I probably wouldn't have been good for you. Those were my wild and wooly days."

"Was it a bad marriage from the start?"

"Probably. We married for the wrong reasons. Ah, here's our soup."

Saved by the bell again, she thought. Getting information out of him was like trying to saddle a greased pig. Must have been all those years as a cop that made him so averse to personal disclosure. And he was about as forthcoming with his feelings as the Sphinx. That male thing, she supposed. In spades.

The soup was thick, rich and flavorful, and the entrée that followed was marvelous. She even had a bite of his Panang, which was tasty despite its being fiery enough to sear half the taste buds from her tongue. The service was exceptional. As Cole predicted, she felt stuffed and pampered.

She reached across the table for his hand. "This was fantastic. Thanks for bringing me here. I've had a wonderful time."

He brought her hand to his lips and discreetly flicked his tongue between her knuckles. "The night isn't over yet. And we still have tomorrow."

After he paid the check, Kelly waited outside while Cole spoke privately with Kusa for a few moments. She lingered in front of the flower shop, again admiring the pots of orchids in the window display.

"Like those?" Cole said behind her.

"They're lovely. All of them, but I especially like that one." She pointed to a purple one with several flowers like moths alighted on a long delicate stem. "And that one, the yellow."

"Wait here," he said.

He went inside, and she smiled as she watched the proprietor take the two pots from the window. When he came out a few minutes later, he was sniffing and struggling to carry the two pots and manage his cane. Her heart simply melted. She wanted to throw her arms around him and kiss him and shout her love so loudly that everybody in Houston could hear.

Instead she waited there, grinning. "For me?"

"Naw. I thought Howard and the geezers might like these to brighten up the office at the Twilight Inn."

She laughed. "They might."

He handed the pots to her. "Of course they're yours. The purple one is a phal-ae-nop-sis, and the other one is...uh...isn't. I have the names in my pocket and a brochure with instructions for care and feeding."

"You're a sweetheart," she said, kissing his cheek. "Thank you."

He sneezed. "You're welcome."

"But now you're sneezing. We'll put these on the balcony or leave them in my car as soon as we get home."

"You'll freeze the little buggers' buds off. They like it warm and cozy. And I don't think we have to worry about it. The woman in the shop said that many people with flower allergies aren't affected by orchids—at least not just a couple of small pots of them. My sniffing and snorting is from all the other stuff in there."

"And you braved the sneezy monsters for lil' ol' me," she said in her best Scarlett O'Hara imitation. "I'm hon-ahed, sir."

He chuckled. "As well you should be, madam." He held open the car door for her.

They stopped by a grocery store to get provisions for breakfast. Advertising itself as open twenty-four hours a day, the place was huge and carried everything under the sun. While Kelly gathered fruit and the makings for French toast, Cole went to the pharmacy section to have his antihistamine prescription refilled.

"Did you get coffee?" Cole asked when he caught up with her in the bakery department.

"Yes. And milk. And juice. Just look at all these wonderful kinds of fresh-baked breads to choose from. Can you believe it? I'm in culture shock after being used to Bullock's."

He smiled. "I've never seen anybody get so excited over a few loaves of bread. You know, if you moved to Houston, you could have a different kind of bread every day and eat Thai food to your heart's content."

She glanced up. Was he just teasing or was there more meaning behind his comment? Nothing in his face told her. "Oh, it might be tempting for the shopping, but I'd have to put up with the goshawful traffic and all the rest. Besides, there's the matter of my practice."

"Doctors can open an office anywhere."

"True, but establishing a practice is difficult. And besides," she said lightly, as she selected a brioche loaf, "if I skipped out of Naconiche, who would deliver Sarah Townsend's babies?"

"What's so special about her?"

"She and her husband and their brood live down a pig trail miles from town, and she won't come to the hospital. I have to go there. And last time I got paid with a goat."

He grinned. "What did you do with the goat?"

"Staked it in the backyard until I could find a home for it. Have you ever milked a goat?"

"Is it anything like milking a cow?"

"How should I know? I've never milked a cow. But I learned how to milk a goat."

He laughed. "I would've liked to have seen that."

"No, you wouldn't have. It was not a pretty sight, and I was extremely profane in my comments to Portia."

"Who's Portia?"

"The goat."

His shoulders shook with laughter, and he looped an arm around her neck. "You, Dr. Martin, are a treasure. Let's check out."

TIME PASSED QUICKLY—more quickly than he would have liked—and with one thing and another, their

Sunday breakfast became Sunday brunch. They sat on the couch to eat; Cole had given her the TV tray and put his plate on the coffee table. It was almost twelve o'clock when he mopped up the last of his maple syrup with the French toast Kelly had made.

"Doctor, you are one fine cook," he said, leaning back and patting his belly. "That was the best French toast I've ever eaten."

"Thanks. I'd offer you some more, but it's all gone. You really worked up an appetite."

"After a whole night and morning with you, I had to build my stamina back up."

"Too much woman for you, huh?" She stood and reached for his plate.

He pulled her down into his lap. "That'll be the day." He licked her lips. "You taste like cinnamon and maple syrup."

She licked his. "So do you."

Powerful feelings swelled in his chest, and he rested his forehead against hers. "Why don't we play hooky and hole up here for a couple of weeks? I'll take you to all my favorite places."

"Can't. I have patients scheduled and half a dozen meetings to attend."

"Don't you ever take a vacation?" he asked.

"A day or two here and there. A week in the summer."

"You work too hard."

"My patients need me."

"*I* need you." He kissed her then before he could think anymore about what he'd said. It had popped out out of nowhere.

A distant ringing broke them apart, and he silently cursed.

"Your cell phone," he said. "In the bedroom."

"Not mine, big guy. It's yours. Answer it while I do the dishes."

Muttering, he stomped to his bedroom and picked up his cell. "Hello," he barked.

"Did I interrupt something?" J.J. asked.

"Hell yes. What do you want?"

J.J. laughed. "Sorry about the timing, but we just got out of church, and I wanted to call you before you left Houston. What time are you planning on being back?"

"Oh, about five, I imagine. We'll be leaving in a couple of hours. Kelly has a meeting at six. Why?"

"I have something I want to show you at the four-plex. Swing by there first if you don't mind."

"And if I do?"

"Don't hand me grief, big brother," J.J. said. "Do it anyway. Bring Dr. Kelly, too. Give me a call when you're on the road."

Chapter Sixteen

When Cole pulled into Naconiche late Sunday afternoon, he was tired and his hip was aching. Kelly had followed him in her car, and they'd stopped along the way for coffee and a piece of pie, but the extra workout of the weekend plus the long ride had taken its toll. He really didn't feel like stopping by the fourplex to check out the apartment that afternoon, but he'd promised J.J. that he would.

He parked behind J.J.'s pickup, and Kelly arrived as he was getting out of his SUV. Frank's car was in a slot as well. Visiting Carrie upstairs no doubt.

"I think you overdid it this weekend," Kelly said. "You're limping."

"I'm fine."

"Don't try to play the macho game with me, Cole. I'm a doctor, remember?"

He hooked his arm around her neck and nuzzled her ear. "I thought macho turned you on."

"There's macho and then there's macho."

He grinned. "Ah, that makes sense."

"Don't try to divert me," she said. "I'm like a bulldog."

"I'm a little tired and stiff from the long car trip. How about that?"

"Better. A long soak in the tub would help."

"Want to join me?"

The door to one of the downstairs apartments opened and J.J. stepped out. "Hey, you two, quit making out in the parking lot and get in here."

"Cork it, J.J.," Cole said. "What's so all fired important that I need to look at?"

"Come on in and see." J.J. held the door for them to enter.

Mary Beth, Carrie and Frank all yelled, "Surprise!"

Cole looked around. "Is it somebody's birthday?"

"No, silly," Mary Beth said, grabbing his arm and leading him farther into the room. "It's a housewarming for your new place. We furnished it and moved you in while you were gone. Like it?"

"Sure. Where'd all this stuff come from?"

"Well," Mary Beth said, "the recliner is the same one you had at the Twilight Inn, and the couch is rented from a place in Travis Lake."

"The TV is an extra one of mine," Carrie said. "And the kitchen table and chairs are ones I had stored in Frank's barn."

"The coffee table is an old trunk that was stored out there, too," Frank said, "and the bedroom furniture is from one of the guest rooms at my place that nobody uses."

"Carrie and I bought the end tables, bookcase and lamps at a thrift store in Travis Lake," Mary Beth said. "And the pictures and accessories are on loan from Florence Russo. That woman has more things in storage than we have in our whole house.''

''Everybody contributed to the kitchen necessities and linens,'' Carrie said, ''including your mother.''

''The place comes with a stove, a microwave and a refrigerator,'' J.J. said, ''and a stacking washer and dryer. Your clothes are in the closet, your socks are in the drawers and your shaving kit's in the bathroom. So I guess you're set.'' He rocked back on his heels and grinned. ''Close you mouth, big brother. You're catching flies.''

''Thanks, all of you,'' Cole said. ''I don't know what else to say.''

'''How about a beer?' might do,'' Frank said

''I don't have any beer.''

''Yes, you do,'' Frank said. ''We brought it.''

Cole passed on the beer in favor of a pain reliever and a soft drink, and Kelly took a Coke, as well. ''I have a hospice center committee meeting,'' she told them, ''and I wouldn't want Reverend Whitaker to smell essence of hops on my breath.''

Everyone else had beer, and while they were drinking, Kelly excused herself to leave for her appointment.

''Hang on a minute and let me get my stuff out of your car,'' Cole said. ''J.J., Frank, can you guys give me a hand?''

Outside, when J.J. hefted the duffel from Kelly's trunk, he said, ''Good God, what have you got in here?''

''My rock collection. And the garment bag is mine, too. Frank, would you get that other bag and the small cooler out of my car?''

"And what are you going to get, Sergeant?" Frank asked him.

"I'll carry the laptop." He turned to Kelly. "Can you come by after your meeting?"

"If it isn't too late. I'll give you a call."

On their way back inside, Frank said, "I can't tell you how glad I am to have you living here. Now if somebody sees my car here too often, they won't know who I'm visiting."

"Glad to be a handy cover."

"Works both ways," Frank said. "At least this place is off the main drag. Everybody in town passes by the Twilight Inn to check out the cars parked in front."

"With their stopwatches," J.J. added. "Been there."

After they carried his belongings inside, his brothers and their ladies soon dispersed. And none too soon. He appreciated what they'd done to fix up the place and move him in, but he was bone weary. He sank into the recliner to relax and ease his aching body.

It seemed that he'd barely closed his eyes when his cell phone rang.

"You sound sleepy," Kelly said. "Did I wake you?"

"I just dozed a little. What time is it?"

"Seven-thirty," she said. "Our meeting was just over. Tell you what, you're tired and I'm tired so let's both call it a night. Do you have food for dinner?"

"I think they stocked the fridge, and I still have the leftover eggs and milk and stuff we bought in Houston. I won't starve."

"I had a wonderful time," she said. "And thanks again for the orchids. I've already found perfect spots for them."

"You're welcome. Call me when you have a break."

"Maybe Tuesday."

Tuesday was too damned far away, he thought after they'd hung up. He already missed her. It wouldn't take much to get addicted to Kelly.

He rummaged around in the kitchen and found a plate of what looked like his mother's chicken-salad sandwiches in the refrigerator. He ate two of them with a glass of milk.

His nap had taken the edge off his exhaustion, so he unpacked his clothes in the bedroom. At least now he could wear a dress shirt and tie to his temporary job and look more professional. Back in the living room, he lifted the big duffel onto the trunk in front of the couch, unzipped it and started putting books into the small bookcase that the TV sat on. He could have used a few more, but he'd brought back the ones most critical to his research. At least now when he wasn't busy at the police station or with other things—like Kelly—he could use his time productively. He wasn't cut out to be a couch potato.

MONDAY WAS A KILLER for Kelly, and Tuesday wasn't much better. There was a stomach virus going around. She was leaving her office when she got a call from the ER. Dixie Russo's second from youngest had stuck half a bottle of capers up his nose, and Kelly rushed to the hospital.

"Well, at least I can say Eddie's a connoisseur,"

Dixie said later when the child's nasal cavities were clear. "The two others of mine who tried it used dried black-eyed peas."

Kelly laughed. "Your attitude amazes me."

"Better to laugh than go bonkers. See you Thursday night at exercise class."

After Dixie and the boy had left, Kelly was at the desk writing up her report when one of the ER nurses approached and said quietly, "I can't locate Dr. Watkins. Could you check out one of his patients that just came in?"

"Sure. What's the problem?"

The nurse glanced around, then whispered, "An *accident* she said. It's Mrs. Iverson. She's having trouble breathing."

Kelly hurried into the room where Mrs. Iverson was. The woman was pale and trembling. "Your doctor isn't available right now. I'll help if I can. What happened?"

"I…uh…fell on the back steps. So clumsy of me. It hurts here when I breathe." She put her hand under her left breast.

After examining her briefly and noting the deep bruising on her torso, Kelly ordered an X ray.

No ribs were cracked or broken, surprising considering the lick she had to have sustained. Kelly gave Mrs. Iverson an injection as well as a prescription for pain medication and instructions for care. "Is someone with you?" she asked the woman.

Mrs. Iverson, still pale and shaken, said. "I'm alone. I drove here by myself."

"You don't need to be driving. May I call Mr. Iverson to pick you up?"

"No! I mean, he's...out of town. I can drive. I'll be fine."

"I'd really prefer that you didn't. Let me drop you off. I'm on my way home."

Mrs. Iverson hesitated, then reluctantly agreed.

Later, after Kelly helped the woman into her car, she said, "Will Mr. Iverson be home tomorrow? You're going to be very sore, and you may need some help managing the essentials. I really don't like for you to be alone tonight. Perhaps we could call a friend or a neighbor."

The injured woman began to cry softly.

Kelly squatted beside her. "What's wrong?"

Mrs. Iverson shook her head. "I don't have any friends."

"Tell you what," Kelly said. "I have an empty guest room. You can come home with me."

Mrs. Iverson's shoulders sagged. "Oh, thank you. The Lord will bless you for this."

Taking a patient home with her, especially Warren Iverson's wife, was stupid, but it wasn't the first stupid thing she'd done in her life. Something fishy was going on, Kelly thought as she drove into her driveway. She didn't believe that Beulah Iverson's injury was from a fall down the steps, but she couldn't speculate further without more information.

Naturally, the notion that her husband had done this to her flitted through Kelly's mind. That's all she needed now—getting into the middle of Iverson's family violence. Not that she wouldn't love to hang the sanctimonious old goat out to dry, but if his wife stuck to her accident story, there wasn't much to be done about it.

Except to keep her safe for the night. Which she was doing. Naconiche didn't have a women's shelter. It was past time that they did. That was going to be her next project.

She fed Beulah some chicken soup and tucked her into the guest room bed. That done, she called Cole.

"You sound preoccupied," she said. "You're not still at the police station are you?"

"No, I'm at the apartment shuffling papers. Want to come over and distract me?"

"I'd love to, but I'm beat."

"Want me to come there and massage your feet?" he asked, his tone suggesting more.

"Sounds heavenly, but I have a guest."

"Oh?"

"A female guest," she said. "How about I buy you lunch tomorrow at the tearoom?"

"You're on. And I'll buy you dinner in Travis Lake. I hear that a new Thai restaurant just opened there."

"That's fabulous. I can't wait. I'll see you at the tearoom at twelve-fifteen or so."

After she hung up, Kelly traced the phone with her finger. Their time together in Houston had spoiled her. She wished Cole were here to soak in a bubble bath with her and massage her feet...and other things.

ON WEDNESDAY MORNING Cole was looking over the preliminary autopsy report when Ham Rayburn came rushing into the chief's office at the station.

"Sir," the young policeman said, waving a sheet of paper. "I've found out something important."

"Aren't you supposed to be handling traffic for that funeral this morning?"

"He's already in the ground. We were on our way to the cemetery when—"

"Who is *we?*"

"Emma Ann and me. Now I know she wasn't supposed to be riding in the patrol car, but that piece of junk she drives wouldn't start, and the whole procession left the funeral home without her. I hated for her to miss the graveside services, since the deceased was her great-uncle and all—or was it her great-great?"

"Cut to the chase, Ham."

The kid frowned. "There wasn't a chase. We drove real slow."

Cole rubbed his forehead. "Get on with the story."

"Okay, so I gave Emma Ann a lift to the cemetery. She was going to get a ride home with her folks, since I didn't plan to stay for the burial service. That's when she saw the picture."

"What picture?"

"This picture of our victim's left shoe, the one we found down by the creek. You remember you gave me a copy of the picture and told me to check with the shoe places in town to see if anybody recognized it."

"I remember. Nobody did."

"Well, I still had that picture in the front seat of the squad car when Emma Ann got in. She had to move it to keep from sittin' on it, and she said, 'What are you doin' with a picture of my aunt Reba's tennie shoe?' And I said, 'It's not your aunt Reba's tennie shoe.' And Emma Ann said, 'I guess I know Aunt Reba's shoe when I see it. It's an original. Mama and

Aunt Reba and Mabel Fortney and one or two others took a shoe painting class down at the I'm Crafty Shop a year or two ago.'''

"Who is Aunt Reba?" Cole asked.

"Reba Conroy, you ought to remember her. Hefty woman. Big hair a kind of funny red color. Her husband Elton owned the tie yard before he died. Worst busybody in town."

"Elton?"

"No. Emma Ann's Aunt Reba. Emma Ann said she'd ask her aunt about the shoes, but I told her to keep out of it. This is police business. Want me to go question Mrs. Conroy, Chief?"

"No, Ham. I want to you go patrol in front of the high school. It's almost lunchtime and the speed demons will be out. I'll question Mrs. Conroy."

When Ham reluctantly left, Cole checked the directory for Reba Conroy's phone number and address. He called and didn't get an answer. If she was Emma Ann's aunt, no doubt she had attended the family funeral and wasn't home yet. He turned back to the report he'd been reading.

KELLY CALLED HER HOUSE on her way to lunch, and Gladys answered.

"You just caught me," Gladys said. "I was on my way out the door."

"Is Mrs. Iverson still there?"

"She lit a shuck this morning not a half hour after you left. Ate about two bites of breakfast and called the cab. Poor lamb. That husband of hers has been mistreating her something awful. She didn't say much, but I could tell from her manner. Haven't I been in that same boat? Takes one to know one, I always say. I told her that I'd done some studying and some praying since Homer left with his floozy, and the Lord revealed to me that it was wrong for a man to dishonor and abuse his mate, and a wife didn't have to stay around and put up with such carrying on.

"Dr. Kelly, I looked her right in the eye and said, 'A woman is contributing to her husband's sins if she doesn't remove herself from his abominable ways.' It was right then she got a gleam in her eye, put down her fork and called the cab."

"Do you know where she went?" Kelly asked.

"Didn't say. I can ask my cousin where he dropped her off if you want me to."

"That's not necessary. Thanks, Gladys."

Cole was just getting out of the car when Kelly arrived at the Twilight Tearoom. He looked especially handsome in a sport coat, dress shirt and tie. She loved the smile that spread over his face when he spotted her. She wanted to run to him and throw herself into his arms—an idea she couldn't act on because Warren Iverson pulled in behind her, honking his horn. She was barely out of the seat when her nemesis came charging toward her, red-faced and hyperventilating.

"Dr. Martin! I demand to know what you've done with my wife."

"Done with her? I haven't done anything with her," Kelly told him.

Iverson grabbed her arm and stuck his face in hers, his fury scorching the air between them. "Don't hand me that! Eyewitnesses told me that you left the hospital with her last night.''

"Hold on just a minute, Warren,'' Cole said, removing the hand that gripped Kelly and easing between them. "Who stepped on your tail?''

Iverson looked up at Cole, and up. The smaller man instantly checked his rage. He deflated like a cheap air mattress. "I'm upset,'' he told Cole, his voice almost a whine. "My wife isn't home, and someone told me she had an accident while I was out of town.''

"I treated her yesterday evening at the emergency room,'' Kelly said, "and, since I didn't want her to drive herself home, she ended up spending the night in my guest room. According to my maid, she left about nine this morning.''

"Why were *you* treating her?''

"Because I'm a *doctor*. Because Dr. Watkins wasn't available, and I was.''

"Satisfied?'' Cole asked gruffly.

It was obvious Mr. Iverson wanted to say more— a lot more—but Cole's presence had muzzled him. As bullies do when they're confronted with someone who can't be intimidated, he sniffed, wheeled and hurried back to his monstrous luxury car.

"God, what a jerk!'' Cole said.

"You've got that right,'' Kelly said. "I sometimes think that the highlight of his day is giving me grief. Did you notice that he didn't inquire about his wife's condition?''

"I noticed. Is she okay?''

"She didn't require hospitalization.''

"What happened?'' Cole asked.

Kelly tucked her arm in his. "I wonder what the special is today? I'm starved."

Cole chuckled. "In other words, it's none of my business."

"I would never say anything so crass."

He kissed her nose and grinned. "Oh, yes, you would. Let's go check out the menu."

Inside they found the usual lunch crowd, but there was one empty table in the middle of the room and Florence Russo, who worked as a part-time hostess, seated them.

"I understand that I have you to thank for the loan of some doodads for my apartment," Cole said to the tall, gray-haired woman.

Florence smiled. "Glad to help. I have tons of doo-dads in my storage building. The special today is southwest chicken. And it's scrumptious. But so is the ham and avocado sandwich according to those who've eaten it."

When Florence left, they discussed the merits of the various offerings on the chalkboard menu, and when the waitress came with their usual raspberry tea, Cole ordered chicken and Kelly opted for the soup-sandwich combo.

"Do you know Reba Conroy?" Cole asked.

"Sure. Why do you ask?"

"I need to talk to her."

"She's right over there." Kelly nodded to a spot over his shoulder. "In the purple."

When he turned, Mrs. Conroy wiggled her fingers at him, heaved herself from the booth where she was sitting and hurried over.

"Why, Cole Outlaw!" the woman gushed, her

voice carrying through the room. "I haven't seen you in ages and ages. Have you forgotten me? I'm Lila Sue and Rodney Conroy's mother."

Cole pushed back his chair and stood. "Mrs. Conroy, it's good to see you again. How are you? And Lila Sue and Rodney?"

"Fine. Just fine. Keep your seat," she said, motioning for him to sit down and taking a chair at the table for herself. "Lila Sue lives in Mobile, Alabama, and has three boys. Rodney is in the Air Force. He married a girl from Japan. Sweet little thing. Doesn't speak much English. Emma Ann tells me that you need to interrogate me about that corpse Wally Gaskamp's dog found—" she leaned closer '——and *my* tennie shoe."

It seemed as if everybody in the tearoom stopped dead still, then turned to listen.

Chapter Seventeen

Cole wanted to stuff a sock in Reba Conroy's mouth. Since that wasn't an option, he said quietly, "I would like to question you, but not here. Could we make an appointment for me to come by your house or for you to drop by the station?"

"Oh, no need for that," Reba said, fluffing her mound of orange hair. "I can tell you everything I know in a minute and a half. Do you have that picture with you?"

Cole started to tell her no to shut her up, then thought, *Hell, this is Naconiche, not Houston.* There were no secrets here. He pulled a folded copy from inside his jacket and handed it to her.

"A little worse for wear, but that's my shoe, all right. I painted it in a jungle motif. See, I divided it into sections like a crazy quilt and colored each one like a different animal print. This is zebra," she said, pointing to the toe, "and this is tiger, and this is leopard. Or is that the cheetah? I never could tell much difference to tell you the truth. I only wore them once. Decided they made me look like a hippie."

"What happened to them?"

"Donated them to the church rummage sale, not last December, but the one before. We have a big sale every year on the first Saturday in December to raise money for missions."

"Do you have any idea who bought them?"

"No, but Mabel Fortney might know. She was in charge that year. Mabel!" she called to the woman sitting at the cash register, motioning her over.

Forks were suspended as everybody in the restaurant watched the woman walk to the table. "Need something?" Mabel asked.

"I'd like to talk with you later," Cole said.

"No need to wait till later when she's here right now," Reba said. "Mabel, do you remember who bought my jungle tennie shoes, the ones I painted when a bunch of us took that class at the craft shop? I donated them to the rummage sale the year you ran it."

"Lord, no. We sold hundreds of things that day."

"Thank you anyhow," Cole said, relieved that the investigation would no longer be conducted in public. "I'll check with you another time to see if you remember something that might help."

Out of the corner of his eye, he caught Kelly with her lips pressed tightly together. She wasn't laughing, but her eyes were.

"Now I don't remember who bought them," Mabel said, "but I remember who I saw wearing them after that."

"Who?" Kelly and Reba asked at the same time. Cole wanted to throttle them both. So much for proper procedure.

"That waitress who used to work here when this

place was the Tico Taco. You must have noticed, Reba. She wore them all the time.''

"I never saw her. Of course, I never ate here then, either. Mexican food gives me gas something awful. I think it's the cumin. What was the woman's name?''

"I don't remember,'' Mabel said. "I'm not sure that I ever knew, but she had a big tattoo of a dragon on her arm.'' She glanced to the register where a group was waiting. "Be right there!'' She hurried away.

"Her name was Rita,'' Curtis, one of the domino geezers, said. He and Will, another of the old guys, were sitting two tables over.

"No,'' Will said. "It was Nita. And her husband's name was Pete, as I recall. Didn't know their last names. I used to come in all the time for enchiladas. Weren't half-bad.''

"There you go,'' Reba said. "You think that was the waitress's body down by the creek? Reckon she was *murdered?*''

"It's too soon to speculate,'' Cole said. "We'll need to investigate further before we can determine that.''

"Just imagine,'' Reba said, rising. "Murdered while she was wearing my jungle shoes. Wait until I tell the girls at circle tomorrow morning.''

Cole gave up trying to control the situation. After Reba left, he said to Kelly, "You have any information to add?''

She grinned. "I didn't think the enchiladas were half-bad, either.''

Cole muttered a string of expletives.

An older lady sitting at the next table leaned over

to him and said softly, "Your mother wouldn't appreciate hearing you use language like that."

"Sorry, ma'am," he said.

"My brother, Dwight Murdock, can give you information about the former tenants of this establishment," she whispered. "I believe he handled Marjorie Bartlett's business affairs."

"Thank you, ma'am. I'll check into it."

"This is so exciting," said the girl who served their lunch. "Being a part of a police investigation and all. If I hadn't seen that picture in Ham's patrol car, none of this would have happened."

"You must be Emma Ann," Cole said.

"Yes, sir, I am. And you don't have to thank me. I was glad to help. Let me get you a refill on that tea."

By the time they ordered dessert, the crowd had thinned considerably. J.J. came in, hung his hat on the rack by the door and strolled over to them. "Dr. Kelly. Cole. Heard you got a lead on our creek body."

"Where'd you hear that?" Cole said.

"Half the folks in town are talking about Reba Conroy's jungle shoe." J.J. winked. "And Nita, the waitress with the dragon tattoo."

Cole made an exasperated sound, and Kelly chuckled. "The other half will be talking about it tomorrow," she said. "Billy Joe Milstead was sitting at the table behind you. And he was taking notes."

"Billy Joe Milstead?" Cole said. "I remember him. He was a friend of Sam's. Quiet, scrawny kid with thick glasses and zits."

"I'm not surprised you didn't recognize him," J.J.

said. "He's beefed up considerably, and the zits are gone. Nowadays he's the editor of the *Naconiche Tribune,* and it comes out on Thursdays."

Cole muttered another string of expletives.

J.J. laughed. "Best to stay on the good side of Billy Joe. He's a pretty good writer."

"Our little weekly has won some prestigious awards, and everybody in this county and the next reads it," Kelly added.

"I'll remember that. I know who Dwight Murdock is, but can you tell me who Marjorie Bartlett is?"

Emma Ann served J.J. a glass of tea. "Mary Beth saved you some chicken if that's what you want, Sheriff. The soup's gone."

"Chicken's fine."

"I'm glad you agreed," Mary Beth said as she approached with two plates. "That's what I brought. May I join you?"

J.J. hopped up grinning. "Shore 'nough, sweet thang." He gave his wife a quick kiss across the table. When Mary Beth had greeted everyone and was seated, J.J. said, "Cole just asked about your cousin Marjorie Bartlett."

"Would this have anything to do with the waitress from the Tico Taco?" Mary Beth asked.

"How did you guess?" Cole said.

Mary Beth grinned. "We got all the juicy details in the kitchen. Most excitement we've had around here since Buck dropped his chef's hat in the deep fryer. Marjorie Bartlett was my cousin, and I was her closest relative. She owned the restaurant and the motel until she died and they came to me. It was because of my inheritance—and I use the term loosely—that

Katy and I returned to Naconiche. The motel was falling down, and the people who had leased the restaurant—it was then a Mexican food place called the Tico Taco—had skipped out owing back rent. I didn't know the couple, but luckily for me they left in such a hurry that Katy and I had food to eat while we lived here.''

"Here?" Cole said. "You *lived* in the restaurant."

"It wasn't so bad," she said.

"Nearly worried me to death," J.J. added. "Her leg in a cast and sleeping in a leaky restaurant with a kid."

"It all turned out well," Kelly said.

"Very well, thanks to J.J. and all the friends who pitched in to help fix up the place," Mary Beth said. "Dwight Murdock was my cousin's attorney and handled her business affairs—such as they were. I'm sure that he probably has information about the couple who leased the restaurant. Shall I have him check?"

"If you don't mind," Cole said. "I would appreciate it. When did they skip town?"

"About this time last year," Mary Beth said. "Maybe a month or so later. Let me get us some more tea."

After she left, Cole said, "I swear I don't know why the mayor asked me to handle this. He could have called a town meeting and solved the whole thing."

J.J. laughed. "Get used to it. We don't do things around here like they do in the big city."

"That's for sure. Of course, you don't find many bodies lying around here, either."

"Only at the funeral home," J.J. said. "I'd have

to check with Pop to be sure, but I don't think we've had a murder in the county in seven or eight years.''

"Not much to keep a homicide cop busy,'' Cole said.

"Nope, but there are other compensations.'' J.J. winked at Kelly. "Word is that, after his heart surgery laid him low, the police chief has about decided to retire. You interested in having the job? The mayor would be tickled to have you.''

Cole snorted. "Are you nuts? I'd be climbing the walls in a month. Besides, I'm still technically employed by HPD, and I don't want to blow my pension for a job running a six-man police department.''

Mary Beth came back with dessert and a pitcher of tea. "Cole, I called Dwight, and he's going to go through his files and find all the information he has on the couple who ran the Tico Taco. He'll drop it by the station in the morning.''

"Great. Thanks, Mary Beth.''

IN HER BEDROOM that afternoon Kelly lay on her stomach next to Cole. Her chin was on his chest, and she blew gently on a tuft of dark hair around his nipple, watching the movement of the hair and the hardening of his nipple.

"What are you doing?'' he asked.

"Playing and thinking.''

He drew a line down her spine with his fingers. "What are you thinking about?''

She pressed her cheek against his chest, laid her hand gently over his healing scar and decided to go for it. "About how much I love you. About how much I'll miss you when you leave Naconiche.''

His fingers stopped. For a moment he didn't seem

to breathe. She could feel his heart pounding against her cheek.

"Say that again."

"I'm going to miss you," she murmured.

He lifted her chin and looked deeply into her eyes. "Not that part. The first part."

"The part about loving you? I do, you know. And I think you love me whether you'll admit it or not."

A smile spread slowly across his face, and he brushed her lips with the tip of his finger. "Oh, I'll admit it. I think it dawned on me sometime when I wasn't looking that I'm crazy in love with you."

She beamed and jumped to her knees. "You are?"

"I am."

She grabbed a pillow and whopped him with it. "Why didn't you tell me, you louse?"

Laughing, he crossed his arms to fend off the blows. "I'm telling you now."

"Tell me again."

"I love you."

She hit him again. "Louder."

"I love you!" he shouted.

"That's better." She threw herself on him and kissed him with all the passion and joy that was in her.

He returned her passion, and the lovemaking that followed was the sweetest they'd ever shared. His kisses were more profound, his caresses more tender; his entry came with a new wonderment, and she felt complete when they were joined.

"Oh, I love you," he murmured as they moved together.

"And I love you," she whispered as she went soaring.

LATER, WHEN SHE STARTED to get up, Cole said, "Where are you going, darlin'?"

"To get some orange juice. Want a glass?"

"No, but I wouldn't mind a cup of coffee."

"I'll make a pot," she said, pulling on a robe.

"I'll help."

He located his underwear and put on the snug pair of boxer-briefs. Red, she noticed. And extremely sexy.

Following her to the kitchen, he said, "I'm hungry. Got any cookies?"

"Gladys may have made some. We'll check."

"Where are the cats?" he asked, looking around.

"Alas, Rocky and Pierre have deserted me, kitty litter and all. They've moved in with Gladys—permanently, it seems. She pampers them more than I do. And she needs the company they provide. I'm reduced to visiting them occasionally."

"You mean I took an antihistamine for nothing?"

She kissed him and laughed. "There's probably enough lingering dander around here to justify it."

While he peeked in the cookie jar and rummaged through the pantry, she rhythmically measured grounds into the coffeepot with the little brown scoop. She felt like dancing, like twirling around on pointe and laughing as she went. He loved her! Knowing it made her absolutely giddy.

Was now the time to tell him?

No, she thought. She wanted the luxury of savoring this new awareness between them before she introduced another factor into their unseasoned relationship. While they had finally admitted that they loved each other, neither of them had mentioned any sort of lasting commitment. She wanted to feel him out a bit on his long-term plans for them.

The thought of living in Houston again made her shudder. How could she simply walk away from her practice and the hospice project? People depended on her. Who would start a women's shelter if she didn't? She loved living in Naconiche, but it was obvious that Cole hated the idea. For a moment at lunch, she thought J.J. had come up with the perfect answer— an offer for Cole to stay and be the police chief. She could have cried when Cole immediately nixed that possibility. Even the logistics of where to live was a major problem if they continued any kind of relationship, much less marriage. One of them would have to give.

She hated the idea that he might feel trapped into marriage with her if she told him about the baby at this point.

On the other hand, he had a right to know that he was going to be a father.

This weekend, she thought. I'll tell him then. Or maybe next week for sure. She couldn't wait too much longer or she would be showing. Warren Iverson would blow a gasket if he knew she was pregnant and unmarried. The question of her staying in Naconiche might be moot. Iverson would find a way to revoke her hospital privileges, tie her to the World War I memorial on the courthouse lawn and brand her with a cattle iron from one of the ranches in the county.

"Darlin', I think that coffee may be a mite strong. You've put about twenty scoops in the basket."

She laughed and dumped the grounds back into the can and started over. "My mind was on other things."

He brushed aside her hair and kissed the back of her neck. "What kind of things?"

"Does your family have a cattle brand?"

"Double O Bar. What made you think of that?"

"I was thinking of getting a tattoo on my fanny," she said, covering quickly. "Did you find any cookies?"

"No to the tattoo. Yes to the cookies."

"*No?* Are you trying to tell me what I can do to my own fanny?"

"Now don't go all huffy on me, sweetheart." He cupped her bottom. "I have a stake in this lovely derriere now, and you can't improve on perfection."

"You sweet man." She turned and draped her arms around his neck. "My derriere is far from perfection. A tattoo might help. A dainty butterfly maybe. Or a dragon. Wonder where Nita got her dragon?"

"I couldn't begin to guess. Tell you what. Let's find some of those temporary ones, and I'll put one of those on you."

"It's a deal." She grabbed the orange juice from the fridge and drank straight from the bottle. "Let's get dressed and go find one."

"I didn't mean right now. What about my coffee?"

"You don't need any coffee." She thrust the orange juice bottle at him. "Have some juice. Have a cookie, but not more than one. You'll spoil your dinner. I'm going to take a quick shower and get dressed. We have to meet the others in an hour and a half anyhow."

"I can't believe you invited half the town to go to dinner with us."

"I didn't invite half the town," she said. "I invited your brothers and Mary Beth and Carrie. They like Thai food as much as we do."

"J.J. was just talking to hear his lips flap. He wouldn't know Panang from a cow patty. He doesn't eat anything that isn't covered in cream gravy or catsup."

"His tastes have matured since Mary Beth came back and opened the Twilight Tearoom," she said, giving him a peck on the cheek. "Now don't grouse about it. We'll have fun. Where do you think we can find a temporary tattoo?"

He shrugged. "Probably at a regular tattoo parlor or more likely a toy store. Kids get them all the time."

"I know just the place—a little trailer on the way to Travis Lake. It has a huge red neon sign across the front, and there are usually about half a dozen motorcycles parked in front—the big, bad-looking kind with lots of silver stuff on them. I've always wanted to stop there."

"Let's try the toy store first."

KELLY AND COLE WERE RUNNING a wee bit late. The other two couples were already seated and having wine and beer when they arrived at the new Thai restaurant.

"Where've you been?" J.J. asked. "We were getting ready to order without you."

"You wouldn't know what to order without me," Cole said, thumping his brother on the head.

Kelly waved a sack she carried. "Sorry, but we had to go two places to find these, and then I had a hard time deciding."

"What did you get?" Carrie asked.

"Temporary tattoos. We're going to put one on my butt."

Frank snorted a laugh and spewed beer halfway across the table.

Chapter Eighteen

Cole was sitting in the chief's office trying to get some work done, but Kelly kept sneaking into his mind. He got tickled every time he thought about the night before when she announced that she was putting a tattoo on her butt—and about Frank spraying beer on everybody. He guessed it was hard for Frank to think of his children's doctor, hell, *his* doctor talking about such things. J.J. had thought it was a hoot, and before the evening was over, Kelly had given everybody a tattoo to take home. She had plenty. She'd bought more than a dozen.

Too bad he would have to wait until this weekend to try them out. Looked like he was going to be spending the next couple of days in south Louisiana trying to verify the identity of their homicide victim. The autopsy report had made that definite. It was a homicide. A blow to the skull.

Dwight Murdock had dropped an envelope by the station for Cole first thing that morning. Pete and Nita turned out to be Evert and Juanita Fontenot, and his brother was listed as next of kin. A phone call to the brother's number in New Iberia, Louisiana, was answered by the brother's wife.

"Pete Fontenot was one of the sorriest creatures to ever walk this earth," she'd said. "I hated to see him come back down here and be a bad influence on my husband. Somebody took care of that worry for me, though. He got killed in a bar fight last summer. He's dead and buried in the graveyard next to his mama."

"What about his wife Nita?"

"Nita didn't come back with him. Got sick of his ways and left him, I figured."

"Do you know of any way I might try to find her or some of her family?" Cole had asked.

"Let's see. She was a Herbert. I believe she's got some kin in Lake Charles. A brother maybe. Or a sister. Wasn't much to any of that family, either, if you ask me."

Cole had talked to the police chief in New Iberia, and he had confirmed that Evert Fontenot a.k.a. Pete Fontenot had been killed in a fight last July the Fourth. The chief agreed to fax him all the information they had on Fontenot and the incident. He didn't know anything about a wife.

Using an online directory, Cole checked phone numbers for Herberts in Lake Charles. There were over two hundred of them. He'd get more done if he went there and worked through their police department. He made a call to Lake Charles PD, then one to Mayor Fletcher for travel funds. Too bad Kelly couldn't drive over with him. He called and left her a message that he'd be out of town for a couple of days.

Ham Rayburn stuck his head in and waved a newspaper. "Chief, you read the *Tribune* yet? We're front-page news."

"No, I haven't read it. Ham, how would you like to drive me to Lake Charles on business?"

"Lake Charles, Louisiana?"

"Yes."

"Be fine with me. When are we leaving?"

"In about an hour. We'll be gone one night, maybe two."

"I'll have to call Emma Ann and break our date for tomorrow night in case we don't get back. Want me to wear my uniform?"

"No. Wear a sport coat and tie if you have them—and pack light."

Ham grinned. "It's gonna be a plainclothes assignment?"

Cole tried not to roll his eyes. "Sort of. And Ham, don't tell Emma Ann where you're going or what we're doing."

"Gotcha, Chief. Should I buy a shoulder holster for my weapon?"

"Not this time."

He checked several databases for information on the Fontenots, including the driver's license division of DPS, and got a few hits. He printed out his findings, then went home to pack.

KELLY WAS GETTING READY for bed Friday night when the phone rang. She answered.

"Hi, angel."

"Who is this?"

Cole chuckled. "Who would you like it to be?"

"A tall, dark hunk who's been gone too long. When are you coming home?"

"We'll be leaving in the morning about ten, and we should be home by midafternoon. Have anything planned?"

"Not a thing. Want to come over and hang out with me?"

"Sounds good," he said. "Ham just doesn't do it for me."

She laughed. "Have you had a productive trip?"

"Very. I think we've about wrapped up this case, and I'll be out of a job. Looks like our victim was indeed Nita Fontenot, and in all probability her husband Pete killed her, then skipped town, but he's dead and the trail ends. We're going to get a DNA sample from Nita's sister to send to the crime lab for comparison."

"Why do you think he killed her?"

"The motive? Who knows? He was just a hot-headed bastard. Her brother was the one who killed him. The brother had gone looking for Pete to ask about his sister. Seems Pete was drunk and admitted killing the 'two-timing slut.' When the brother cursed him, Pete pulled a knife, and the brother brained him with a beer bottle."

"Lovely story. Nice people."

"Darlin', they're the kind of trash I deal with all the time. Nice people don't commit homicide. Reality isn't like movies where the villain is a Hollywood star. Scumbags and hopheads are the ones who kill each other, and most of the time 'nice' is a facade."

"You sound strange," Kelly said.

"In what way?"

"I'm not sure," she said, trying to choose her words carefully. "There's a hard edge to your voice that makes me uncomfortable."

"I am hard, sweetheart. Nearly twenty years as a cop will do it to you. My job isn't for sissies."

"I can't imagine anyone ever mistaking you for a sissy." She rolled over onto her side. "Hurry home. I miss you."

"I miss you, too, Kelly. I love you, darlin'."

"I love you, Cole Outlaw. With all my heart."

COLE TOOK OFF HIS SHIRT, hung up his pants and stretched out on the motel bed. His hip ached like a son of a bitch. Even with Ham along to do the driving, the trip had been rough on him. Every muscle in him was tighter than a bowstring, and he wanted a drink. He recognized the feelings.

Stress.

In the last couple of days, he'd put on an attitude when he'd knotted his tie and slipped on his jacket. He was back in his cop mode. That was what Kelly had heard in his voice. Being a cop—a good cop— made a person cynical and edgy. Wallowing around in cesspools and witnessing the filth and violence that he had encountered had colored his opinion of human nature. He hadn't formed a high opinion of it.

Being a cop, living under constant stress and fraternizing with the dregs of society took its toll. A lot of his buddies on the force had suffered burnout with the job. And divorce. And alcoholism.

One of his friends had told him that he didn't want to look at life through a cop's eyes anymore. "My wife is an artist,'' Kyle had said. ''When we go to the park and see a tree, she sees beautiful shades of green and birds singing in the branches. I see the litter on the ground and the pedophile lurking behind the trunk. And I drink too much and make her cry all the time for no good reason. Sometimes I think my kids are afraid of me. I'm becoming as big a bastard as the ones we lock up. I'm burned out and burned up. I'm gone.''

Burnout. Was that what had happened to him? Had he lost some of that edge and gotten himself shot? Maybe.

He hadn't realized how stressed out he'd been until he hung around Naconiche for a while. The pace was definitely slower there. His blood pressure had dropped fifteen points.

But, he thought, there was something to be said in favor of stress. For the past couple of days he'd felt back in the groove, energized and alive again. He'd enjoyed the challenge of chasing leads and finding answers, the camaraderie of police officers who spoke the same language that he did—even if it was with a Cajun lilt. So maybe he was a little stressed. It came with the territory.

Besides, being a cop was all he knew. And Kelly filled in all the empty holes he'd had in his life up to now. Loving her and living with her would keep him balanced. He hoped he could convince her to move to Houston—at least until he had his twenty—if and when the doctor released him for duty. Those were big ifs and whens. He was due to report in for an evaluation pretty soon.

WHEN THE KNOCK CAME, Kelly wiped her hands on a dishcloth, hurried to the back door and flung it open. "Hey there, good-lookin'. Get yourself in here."

He stepped inside, opened his arms and she stepped right into them. "Something sure smells good in here."

"Eau de chocolate and onions."

"Interesting combination." He kissed her nose.

"Not together. I've been baking. I made chocolate chip cookies and brownies and earthquake cake, and I just put a meat loaf in the oven. It has onions and bell pepper and tomatoes, so I've covered all the major food groups. Do you like meat loaf?"

"I love meat loaf." He kissed her left eye. "What's an earthquake cake?" He kissed her right eye.

"A sinfully delicious chocolate cake with pecans and coconut and gooey stuff. One of the girls in the office gave me the recipe. Want a piece? I'll turn on the coffee."

"It's not a piece of cake that interests me right now," he said, going for her mouth.

The front doorbell rang.

"Ignore it," he said.

It rang again. And again.

"I'll be right back," she said. "Hold my place."

Her mail carrier stood at the front door. "Afternoon, Dr. Kelly. You've got a certified package you need to sign for."

"Thanks, Loretta," she said as she signed the card. "How are you today? Has your rash cleared up?"

"All gone. That ointment did the trick. You have a good day now."

Kelly brought the thick brown envelope and the rest of the mail back to the kitchen with her. She pitched most of it onto the island, but she stared at the package. "Wonder what this is and who it's from. There's no return name on it, only a post office box in Tyler."

"I know a really good way to find out," Cole said.

She grinned. "Why don't I open it. Will you hold my place a little longer?" She ripped the envelope zipper and pulled out a folder full of papers. A pink sticky note was attached to the front. "It's from Beulah Iverson. She says she's left her husband and thanks for my kindness to her. I'm to use the enclosed material in any way I see fit."

Itching with curiosity, she opened the folder and let out a yelp of laughter. The yelp turned into gales. Every time she looked back at the first page another laugh spewed out.

"What's so funny?"

Kelly couldn't stop laughing long enough to explain. She handed him the folder and he started laughing.

"Good Lord," he said. "I didn't know Warren had it in him."

The first page was a photocopied picture of Warren Iverson, nude, his scrawny bare bottom in the air and a deer-caught-in-the-headlights expression as he gaped over his shoulder at the photographer. The woman he was atop wasn't Beulah.

"He doesn't exactly," she said—and started laughing again.

"Get a load of this one." Cole handed her another picture. "Old Warren is pretty well hung."

They made their way through several pictures and scanned copies of a private investigator's reports. Though not all the photos were quite so graphic, there were a number of them as well as reports suggesting that Iverson had carried on affairs with three different women over the past couple of years.

"That sanctimonious snake!" she said. "I can't believe that all the time he was dealing me misery he was out cavorting around like a tomcat."

Cole picked up one of the photographs and studied it closely. "Do you know this woman?"

She scrutinized it carefully. "She seems vaguely familiar, but I'm not sure who it is."

"Check out the tattoo."

She had to squint to make it out. "It looks sort of like a snake or a—a *dragon?* Is this your waitress?"

"It resembles the picture on her driver's license. Which report goes with this batch of pictures?"

They sorted out the material, and Cole read one of the reports more carefully. "Says here that Warren and Nita were seen together at a motel in Travis Lake less than a week before Pete Fontenot left town."

"Do you think Pete found out about his wife's hanky-panky with Warren Iverson and killed her?" she asked.

"I doubt that we'll ever know, but I need to question Iverson."

Kelly giggled. "I'd love to be a fly on the wall for that. I hope Beulah takes him to the cleaners. Bless her sweet heart for sending this to me. One thing is sure. That jerk will never get on my case again, or I'll threaten to send this to the *Tribune*. I'm not above a little blackmail."

"Sweetheart, that's not a good thing to admit to a police officer."

"Are you going to run me in?"

"Maybe later." Cole set the inflammatory material aside and pulled Kelly back into his arms. "Now, where were we?"

THE MEAT LOAF BURNED while they were otherwise engaged, but the cake and cookies were delicious, and she adored her new tiger tattoo. It was big and colorful, and it made her feel totally decadent. Cole had carefully placed it just above the dimple on her rump, and she growled every time she caught a glimpse of her backside in the mirror.

She'd tried three times to put one on him, but the places she picked were either too hairy or locations of a sort not optimal for transfers. Even so, they'd had great fun trying. They had laughed and loved away the entire afternoon and evening.

A couple of times Kelly had thought about telling him about the pregnancy, but she'd let the moment pass. The two of them had been playful and carefree, and the mood hadn't seemed right to break such serious news.

They'd fixed tomato soup and grilled cheese sandwiches for dinner, then gone back to bed to play Scrabble, watch TV and make love again. She'd slept in his arms, totally content.

The next morning when she opened her eyes, his were already open and watching her. She started to turn toward him when it hit her. Oh, no! This was going to be one of those mornings. She climbed over him and bounded for the bathroom.

"Kelly?" he called after her, but she didn't dare stop.

She barely made it to the commode before the retching started.

"Kelly? Honey, are you all right? Are you sick?"

What a stupid damned question! she thought as she tossed her cookies again.

He knelt beside her on the tile and bathed her face with a damp cloth. "Can I do something?"

She shook her head and waited for the next wave. It didn't come.

She flushed the toilet and sat back on her heels on the cold tile. Cole put his arm around her and bathed her face again. "Do you think it was something you ate?" he asked, sounding worried. "Or maybe a virus?"

"No," she said quietly. "It's morning sickness. I'm pregnant."

"Pregnant?"

She nodded. "I'm going to have a baby."

"When?"

"Sometime in September."

He looked horrified. "You got pregnant last *September?*"

"No, it's *due* in September. I got pregnant sometime in December."

He hugged her to him and rocked her in his arms as they sat naked on the floor. "You about scared the hell out of me."

"Is that all you have to say?"

"Oh, I have a lot to say, darlin'. I just want to make sure you're okay first."

"I'm okay. Once it has passed, I feel fine."

"Then let's go back to bed and get under the covers. My butt's about to freeze on this floor."

She chuckled. "Let me rinse my mouth first."

He helped her up and waited while she rinsed with water, then with mouthwash.

"Let me have a slug of that stuff," he said, reaching for the bottle and making a big show of gargling.

He led her back to bed, propped pillows against the headboard, climbed in and pulled her in after him. When he had her snuggled against him and had arranged the covers, he said, "Now we talk."

"Are you angry?"

"Angry?" he said. "Why would I be angry? We both contributed to this situation. How long have you known about it?"

"For a while."

"Why didn't you tell me sooner?"

"Well, for one thing I wanted to be sure that the fetus would remain intact. Because of some problems I have, pregnancy was supposed to be a problem for me."

"Is everything okay?"

"According to my doctor, everything is fine and it looks like the pregnancy will go to term."

"That's great, darlin'." He kissed her forehead. "How's next Saturday sound to you?"

"For what?"

"For the wedding."

"What wedding?"

"Ours, of course. I figure that ought to be the first thing on the agenda. We can work out the other issues later."

She frowned and sat up. "Not so fast. I'm in no

hurry to get to the altar. Let's work out the other issues, then we'll discuss marriage. Marriage may not even be an option. I'm not trying to trap you. Then there's the problem of your job in Houston and my practice here. Would we have a commuter relationship or is one of us going to move? We have a lot to talk about.''

''I don't feel trapped, and I don't see any reason to complicate things. We love each other. You're pregnant. We get married—the sooner, the better. I'm an old-fashioned guy. I can take the chief of police job here. You can clean out a couple of drawers and a foot of closet space for me, and I'll move in. I'll hold your head while you upchuck, and we'll take those childbirth classes together. Simple.''

Kelly stared at him for a minute, then said, ''Uh-uh.''

Chapter Nineteen

Kelly was as stubborn as a blue-nosed mule, Cole thought as he drove to the police station on Monday morning. They had argued the rest of the weekend about getting married right away, but she wouldn't budge. She wanted them to take their time and be *sure,* she'd said.

Hell, he was *sure.* He loved her. She was pregnant. They got married. Soon. Still seemed simple to him. In fact, now that the news had sunk in on him, he kind of liked the idea of being a daddy.

Then there was the question—the sticking point—of where they would live. Becoming chief of police in Naconiche was a long way from his first choice, and Kelly knew it. That was the problem. She didn't want him to stay here and be unhappy, but by the same token, he didn't want her to have to leave and be unhappy. In the end, they hadn't resolved anything.

He parked in front of the station and went inside, speaking to Ham and the secretary on his way to the office. He'd barely had time to open the case file when his phone rang. It was Dr. John Becker, a professor from Travis Lake Community College, the secretary told him.

"What can I do for you, Dr. Becker?"

"I teach criminal justice at the college," he said. "One of my students brought in a copy of the *Tribune,* and I've been reading about the case you have over there and about you. I was hoping to convince you to come as a guest speaker for one of my classes. It's not often we have someone with your background and experience nearby."

Cole tried to weasel his way out of it, but Becker was persuasive and he caved. "Okay, I'll give it a shot. When?"

"How about tomorrow? You can talk to my ten-thirty Criminal Investigation class and I'll buy you lunch afterward. Just give the students a synopsis of your job in HPD homicide and open it up for questions."

He got directions to the college and hung up. He hoped he didn't make a fool of himself. He'd never done any teaching. Oh, he'd toyed with the idea a little, figuring that he'd have to find something to do after he retired. That was one of the reasons he'd gone back to school himself. Advanced degrees meant extra pay, and the department footed the bill for tuition, so he'd decided: why not?

Taking a course or two at night or on the weekends, he'd earned a master's degree in criminal justice. It had given him something constructive to do and kept him out of bars and out of his ex-wife's hair. After he'd gotten his master's, he'd decided to keep going. He enjoyed learning.

Cole rummaged through a stack of material and

found last Thursday's Naconiche *Tribune*. He never had gotten around to reading it, and he wanted to see what Billy Joe had to say. There'd been a message on his desk that morning from the editor of the weekly. Looking for an interview and update on the case, he suspected. He'd tossed the message.

He was surprised when he finished the story. Although there were a lot of ''sources close to the investigation'' mentioned, the facts were fairly accurate and the piece was well written. Billy Joe had to have interviewed his mother to get the personal information about Cole. It was extremely flattering and made him sound like something just shy of the caped crusader.

Cole had a few more things to do before he wrapped up the case, but the need for his participation was coming to a close. One thing on his list was to interview Warren Iverson as soon as possible. Rather than call for an appointment, he opted for dropping in on him at the candy company.

''He isn't here, Mr. Outlaw,'' his secretary said. ''He's been…fired.'' The woman seemed barely able to keep the glee from her voice. ''Would you like to talk to Mr. Hollis? He's busy with the auditors right now, but I'll see if he has a moment.''

''No. Do you know where I can find Warren?''

A grin escaped despite her best effort. ''I imagine that he's home packing.''

COLE LAUGHED as he recounted the events to Kelly on the phone that night. ''Warren looked like a whipped dog. He was at home packing his personal belongings under the supervision of a couple of Beulah's attorney's associates. From what I gather, she inherited everything from her parents, including the house and the candy company, and not much really belongs to Warren except half of their community property. He'll end up with his car, his clothes and a little cash if he's lucky.''

"Is he leaving town?" she asked.

"He popped off to me about taking an important position in Dallas. But that was before I hit him with questions about Nita Fontenot. He broke down and blubbered like a baby. Seems that Pete Fontenot caught Warren and Nita parked down by the creek one night. Pete was raging mad, dragged Nita out of the car and threatened to bash in Warren's head with a tire iron. Warren was scared witless, lit out and didn't look back. He didn't see either of them after that.''

"Do you think that's when Fontenot killed her?"

"Probably. The timing fits. And Warren said that Nita left some of her clothes in his car, including one sneaker with painting on it. When he learned that they had skipped town, he bagged it and tossed it in the Dumpster behind the convenience store.''

"What a snake!" Kelly said. "Did you believe him?"

"He was too scared to lie. I believed him. And I don't think he'll be bothering you anymore.''

"The town will smell better with him gone. I'm so proud of Beulah for kicking him out. You know I'll bet she would be a great person to head up a committee to start a women's shelter here. She'll need something meaningful to get her out of her shell and keep her occupied.''

"You like to fix more than broken arms and sore throats don't you, darlin'?"

"People are more than body parts to me."

"I know, and I'm very proud of you, Kelly. You're a truly good person. I'll be honored to have you as my wife."

She sniffed. "Don't. You'll make me cry."

"You go to bed and get some rest," he said. "I know you're tired. I'll talk to you tomorrow."

"I love you," she whispered.

"I love you, too."

WHEN KELLY WALKED OUT of the hospital Tuesday evening, Cole was leaning against her car looking like the answer to some woman's prayers.

"Hello, handsome," she said. "Waiting for someone?"

He smiled, and she wanted to melt. "I'm waiting for you. Guess what I have in my car?"

"A crocodile."

"Not even close. I have two big foam containers of Tom Kha Khai."

"Did you make it?

"Not hardly," he said. "I had to be in Travis Lake today, and I picked it up on my way home. I'll tell you about it later. Your place or mine?"

"Mine. If one thing leads to another—and I'm sure it will," she said, wiggling her eyebrows, "I'll already be home to get dressed for work in the morning. Will you rub my feet?"

"I will."

"Oh, bless you. I'll think of some way to compensate.'' She pecked him on the cheek and got in her car.

Once home, she headed for her bedroom to change into something soft and comfy while Cole went to the kitchen to heat their soup and spring rolls.

After they had eaten, Cole sat on the couch and said, ''Come stretch out and I'll massage your feet.''

''You won't hear any arguments from me.'' She plopped down and stuck her feet in his lap.

His thumbs began their magic on her arches, and she moaned. ''That feels *sooo* good. I can't begin to describe it.''

''Aren't you going to ask me why I was in Travis Lake today?''

''Of course I am.'' She scrunched and wiggled her toes as he rubbed. ''Yes. Yes. Right there. Ohhh, heaven. Why were you there?''

''I was a guest speaker at the community college.''

''How neat. What did you speak about?''

''Mostly about investigating homicides. It was a criminal justice class. And you know what? I really enjoyed it. It was a kick. John said I was a natural, but I figured he was just sucking up to me so that I'd come back. He asked me if I'd cover a couple of classes in the morning for a colleague who has to be out.''

''Who's John?''

''John is Dr. John Becker, the professor. We had lunch together and really hit it off. He was on the force in Dallas for several years and got his master's degree a course or two at a time, pretty much the way I did.''

"I didn't know that you had a master's degree," she said.

"Yep. I almost have my doctorate."

"You do? You didn't tell me that."

He shrugged. "I guess it never came up. Going to school gave me something to do, and the department paid for it. I'm down to writing my dissertation now."

"That's wonderful, Cole! Where are you getting your degree?"

"From Sam Houston University in Huntsville. They have one of the finest criminal justice departments in the nation. The hour and a half commute was sometimes a bitch, but with a little juggling of my schedule, I made it okay."

"I'm impressed. To work full-time and manage to get a graduate degree is quite an accomplishment," she said. "I'll bet your family is proud of you."

"I don't think they know about it."

"You didn't tell them? Cole Outlaw! I don't believe it. Sometimes you make a clam look like a chatterbox."

"Don't fuss at me, darlin'," he said, giving her a hangdog look. "You've bruised my ego."

She laughed at that idea. "Poor baby. Come here and let Mama kiss your boo-boo."

He pulled her into his lap. "I'm not sure exactly where my ego is, but we can start here." He brushed his lips across hers.

One thing did lead to another, and he ended up spending the night. Sometime during the wee hours, she awoke, restless.

"Is something wrong?" Cole asked, his voice slurred with sleep.

"I'm fine."

"Then why have you turned over six times in the last two minutes?"

"I've been thinking."

He pulled her close and snuggled. "Too much of that will give you a headache."

"I've been thinking that I really would like to take some time off to be with the baby when it's born. If I moved to Houston with you, I could stay home for two years while you finished the time necessary to qualify for your pension, then maybe we could move back here. If I got bored or if we needed the money, I could work part-time at one of those doc-in-a-box places. It's the sensible thing to do."

"But, honey, you hate Houston. And two years is a long time if you're miserable. You love your practice, and you love Naconiche. It makes more sense for me to take the job here."

"No," she said. "I've decided. I'm going to move to Houston."

"You want to get up and start packing now?"

"No. Go back to sleep."

"When are we going to get married?"

"There's no hurry. We'll talk about it later." She turned over again.

"You seem awful chipper this mornin'," Gladys said. "Wouldn't have anything to do with that car I saw leave here earlier, would it?"

"What car?" Kelly asked.

"You know very well what car, missy. Nonie Outlaw's oldest boy's car. You should know that folks are talkin'."

"Really? And what are they saying?"

"Different things," Gladys said, pouring a glass of orange juice. "Mostly they're wondering if the two of you are going to get married or go on living in sin. Folks have seen the dew on his car here more than once."

"Folks should mind their own business."

"That may be, but that's the way things are around here. And the truth is, Dr. Kelly, I've done a passel of worrying about it myself. I know you've been feeling poorly some mornings, and I don't have to be a doctor to figure out the likely cause of that."

Kelly froze. "I don't know what you're talking about."

"Don't hand me that, young lady. I didn't just fall off a turnip truck."

"You haven't mentioned this to anyone, have you?"

Gladys sniffed and looked affronted. "Certainly not. I'm not much of one to carry tales."

Kelly knew that was true. She stood there for a moment not knowing what to say. She didn't want to lie and deny it; she didn't want to confirm it. Glancing at her watch, she said, "I've got to run, or I'll be late."

"You have plenty of time," Gladys said. "Just sit yourself down and have a decent breakfast. Are you taking vitamins?"

"I *always* take vitamins."

"I have one more thing to say, then I'll hush about it. I grew up in this town, Dr. Kelly, so I know these people. Folks around here will wink at a seven-month baby, but a lot of them won't hold with someone who's looked up to in the community having a baby without a husband. They'll give you grief. That's the way of it. Now, I've spoken my piece. How do you want your eggs?''

Too stunned to say anything, Kelly sat down on a bar stool. Reality hit her between the eyes like a mallet. Warren Iverson wasn't a threat anymore, but there would be others. This was a small town with old-fashioned values. She wasn't a teenager who'd used bad judgment; she was an adult, a role model whether she chose to be or not. She'd known all that before, but it hadn't really sunk in until now.

She was pregnant, and the clock was ticking.

"I'll make scrambled," Gladys said.

"How would people feel about a six-month baby?"

"I'd say you ought to get yourselves down to the county clerk's office today and apply for the marriage license. People will soon be watching your waistline and counting on their fingers."

If she ever wanted to come back to this town without being snickered about, she needed to get into high gear.

Kelly started thinking about all the things she had to do before she could close her practice here. Her first priority was to find a replacement, and it had to be someone who would be compatible with her patients and carry on her work in the hospice program. It would have to be someone with experience since she wouldn't be able to stay very long for a transition. She'd have to sell the house.

Or maybe leasing it would be better.

Or maybe they could keep it and use it for weekend visits.

She ate the eggs Gladys put in front of her and barely tasted them. She had to move quickly or her condition would soon be fodder for the town gossips. She'd already noticed that some of her clothes were getting a wee bit tight.

Her stomach rolled, and she ran for the bathroom.

COLE HAD TAKEN to teaching those classes, to interacting with the idealistic young kids thirsty to learn about law enforcement so that they could go out and do battle with the bad guys. Had he been that fresh-faced and eager when he was eighteen or twenty? Probably. Before he'd burned out from too many years of hitting the wall. Talking to those kids had really juiced him. He was still on an adrenaline high when he came through the door of the Twilight Inn at twelve-thirty. He spotted Kelly sitting at a table with Carrie and J.J. She waved.

"What's going on with you?" J.J. asked. "You're grinning like a wild boar loose in a corn crib."

"It's just gas," Cole said. "What's the special?"

"Beef tips and rice," Carrie said. "With grilled asparagus. That's what Frank and I had. It was really good."

"Where is Frank?" Cole asked.

"He had to get back to court for something," Carrie told him, "and I'm about to leave, too."

"Don't let me run you off," Cole said.

"You're not. I'm trying to get things straightened up in my new office."

Carrie said her goodbyes and left.

Cole looked pointedly at J.J. ''Don't let me run you off, either.''

J.J. grinned. ''You're not. I just got here.''

''How did the classes go?'' Kelly asked.

''What classes?'' J.J. asked.

''Cole filled in to teach a couple of criminal justice classes at the community college in Travis Lake,'' Kelly told him.

''No kidding?'' J.J. said. ''I didn't even know that you could spell criminal justice, Big Buzzer.''

Kelly smiled. ''You might be surprised. Did things go well?''

''Great. What are you having?''

''The chicken salad, I think.''

Just as everyone finished ordering, a man walked up to the table and nodded to J.J. and Kelly. He stuck out his hand to Cole. ''I don't know if you remember me. Billy Joe Milstead.''

''Sam's friend,'' Cole said, quickly shaking his hand. ''Pretty good article.''

''Thanks. I've been wanting to interview you for tomorrow's edition of the paper, but I haven't been able to catch you. I hate to interrupt your lunch, but—''

''Then don't,'' Cole said abruptly.

''Oh, Cole, don't be such a badass,'' J.J. said. ''Pull up a chair and sit down, Billy Joe. How's your mama and 'em?''

''Doing fair.'' He glanced at Cole before he sat down.

Cole gave him a curt nod.

Billy Joe took out a pad and asked several questions about the homicide case, all reasonable, and

Cole answered them as best he could without running off at the mouth. The editor stayed through the meal, never quite pushing too far but being thorough all the same. "Thank you for your time, Cole," he said finally. "And excuse the intrusion, Dr. Kelly." Then he put his pad in his pocket and left before dessert came.

"Newspaper reporters make me nervous," Cole said. "Even the ones on a little weekly like the *Tribune*."

"It's obvious you don't have to run for office to keep your job," J.J. said. "I was right tickled that the *Tribune* endorsed me when I ran. And I hope they will again."

"I'm not cut out to be a brownnose," Cole said.

"A brown—"

"Now boys, boys," Kelly said, chuckling. "Let's play nice."

Her cell phone rang, and when she answered, she frowned. "Thanks, Charlene. I'm on my way." She stood. "I have to go. Sarah Townsend's in labor, and there may be complications."

"I'll go with you," Cole said. "J.J., get the check."

Chapter Twenty

Driving over winding, washed-out dirt roads to the Townsends' place took almost half an hour. Her car wasn't made for rugged terrain. Cole's SUV would have been a better choice, but it was at his apartment, Kelly's supplies were already in her trunk and she didn't want to delay. Mars Townsend had a bad habit of waiting until the last minute to call.

Her nerves were frazzled by the time they arrived at the small unpainted house on a rise by the creek. They were back-to-nature types who eked out an existence on land that had belonged to Mars's maternal grandfather—and had too many babies. Information on birth control was lost on them. She wondered if her replacement would drive to the back of nowhere to do a home delivery. Not many physicians these days would even consider it.

There were complications she discovered right away. Even so, both Mars and Sarah refused to go to the hospital. It was a matter of both money and conviction, and trying to argue would only waste time.

She squeezed Sarah's hand and smiled. ''Just rest if you can. Everything is going to be just fine.''

Kelly took Cole aside and whispered, "Have you ever delivered a baby?"

"Once," he said, "when I was a rookie. But I didn't do much more than just catch it when it came out. Why?"

"Because this baby is turned wrong, and I need some help in turning it right or we might lose both of them. You'll have to give me a hand."

After they'd hurriedly prepared themselves and the area as best they could, the oldest of the children, a seven-year-old girl with an angelic face, was relegated to the front room to supervise the other four. Mars sat at his wife's head, singing softly to calm her, while Kelly and Cole worked and sweated to turn the baby.

Their efforts paid off. Forty-five minutes later, Sarah delivered a big, healthy boy.

When she and Cole started to leave a half hour after that, Mars came running outside, his smile wide. "Don't get off without your pay, Dr. Kelly. One of my sows had a fine litter, and they've just been weaned. I picked out the best one for you."

"A pig?" Kelly said, trying to hide her alarm.

"Yes, ma'am. A Poland China. To my mind, they make the best bacon and pork chops, bar none."

Cole looked as if he would burst out laughing at any minute as she tried vainly to refuse pay. Mars, a proud man, would have none of it. The pig was the best he had to offer.

In the end they drove away with Cole holding the squealing black and white piglet in his lap, a plastic-lined bed pad from her stash in the trunk protecting his clothes.

Thank goodness the piglet quieted down fairly soon, probably from Cole's petting it. "You know," she said, glancing over, "it is kind of a cute little thing. No way am I going to make bacon out of it."

"Pigs make pretty good pets. They're smart, you know. I raised one similar to this one for a school project when I was a kid."

"You weren't allergic to it?"

"Dogs and pigs and horses don't bother me. Only cats."

"It's cute now, but how big will it get?"

Cole grinned. "About four or five hundred pounds I imagine. Maybe twice that."

"That settles it. The pig has to go."

"Want to leave it at Frank's place? I think there's an empty pen there that we can put him in at least temporarily."

"How do you know it's a him?" she asked.

"I looked."

KELLY DROPPED OFF COLE at the tearoom to get his car, and they split up to go home and change. They were going to a dance recital that night. He didn't remember ever going to a dance recital in his life, but several of Kelly's young patients were in it, and she'd promised to attend.

"It won't last more than an hour," she'd said. "Katy and Janey are rose blossoms, and two of Dixie's girls are doing numbers as well as about a half dozen other kids I know. You need to be there for your nieces at least."

He'd thrown up his hands and surrendered.

Kelly loved the kids she treated. And they loved

her. And not just the kids. Kelly was a town treasure. Everybody knew Dr. Kelly, and a lot of them depended on her and put their lives in her hands.

She was a damned good doctor. Better than good. Exceptional. If he hadn't realized it before, he'd been reminded that afternoon. The minute she'd walked into that little shack in the middle of nowhere, it was as if a mantle fell over her, and she became totally focused and professional. He'd been amazed at her strength and skill.

Her patients were her family, and she was fiercely committed to them. How could he expect her to leave Naconiche and the people who needed her. He couldn't. All her talk about staying home for two years was just so much smoke. She didn't belong in Houston. She belonged here. And he had family here who would help them with the baby. And there was Gladys, too.

To hell with his pension and the HPD.

He was going to resign and become the new Naconiche Chief of Police. Since he wouldn't be very busy doing that, no reason why he couldn't stick a playpen in the corner of his office and baby-sit the kid himself. If he could handle a pig, he could handle a baby.

"No," Kelly said. "Absolutely not!"

He found a parking space at the community center, pulled into it and turned to her. "Why not? It makes perfect sense. Truth is, I've about decided that I'm burned out on being a homicide officer anyhow."

"I don't believe you. And what about your pension?"

"I'm going to talk to Jack Russo about that. Since I'm vested, I think I can roll over the account funds into some sort of annuity. And I'll be earning chief's pay here—not much, I grant you, but my future wife's a doctor and everybody knows they're rolling in dough." He grinned.

Kelly snorted. "I wish. Cole—"

"Come on, honey. We're going to be late." He got out and hurried her inside.

The recital was kind of cute. Janey turned the wrong way twice and Katy stopped and waved at J.J. and Mary Beth from the stage. He'd first had his heart set on a boy, but if they had a pretty little red-haired girl, one of these days she'd be up there tiptoeing around in tiny pink slippers.

He found himself grinning and had to check himself from reaching over and patting Kelly's stomach. How long would it be before he could feel a bulge there? He'd have to ask her.

After the recital the whole family gathered downtown at the Double Dip for ice cream.

"Did you see me, Uncle Cole? Did you see me?" Janey asked.

"I sure did. You were great. A perfect rose."

"And me?" Katy asked. "Did you see me?"

"Yep. Another perfect rose. You two were the best of the whole garden."

"Janey turned the wrong way," Katy said.

"Really? I didn't notice."

"See, Katy," Janey said. "I told you. Dr. Kelly said it was practically indefectable."

Holding hands, the girls ran to the counter where his mother was dipping ice cream. He scanned the room for Kelly. He spotted her talking to Carrie and licking a chocolate ice-cream cone.

Dear God, how he loved her. There was nothing he wouldn't do to make her happy. If he had to string paper clips until he was sixty-five, so be it.

"You have the look of a besotted man."

He turned to find his dad standing beside him. "I can't deny that."

"You going to ask her to marry you? Your mother's been wondering."

"I'd marry her right now," Cole said, "if I could get her to agree. I expect we'll be making an announcement soon. But tell Mom to keep that quiet for a while."

Wes Outlaw nodded. "We all think a lot of Dr. Kelly."

FRIDAY MORNING Cole was sitting in the police station finishing some paperwork when the secretary told him Dr. Becker was on line two.

"Good morning, John. How are you?"

"Well, I've got a bit of a problem, and I was hoping you could help me out."

"I will if I can."

"The professor that you substituted for the other day was out of town interviewing for a job in Austin. He got the job, and they would like for him to start right away. He doesn't want to leave us high and dry in the middle of the semester, but this is a once in a lifetime opportunity for him. Is there any possibility that you might consider taking his place?—at least until the end of the term, though we'd prefer to have you full-time. I've talked to the president about it, and we'd like to have you on the faculty.''

A jolt of excitement shot through him. He almost jumped up and shouted. ''When would I start?''

''A week from Monday if you could,'' John said. ''I know this is short notice, but I got the feeling you might like teaching. I think you'd do an excellent job, and your credentials are top-notch.'' He described salary and benefits, which weren't bad for a job that was basically only eight months a year. ''Why don't I give you the weekend to think it over?''

He didn't need the weekend, but he agreed.

Hot damn! What a stroke of luck! Laughing aloud, he smacked a fist into his other hand. Given the choice of returning to HPD, taking the chief's job here and teaching, there was no contest. The idea of teaching full-time fired him up while the other two options were simply a matter of practicality. Teaching would be *fun*.

About to burst with the news, he got in his car and burned rubber all the way to Kelly's office. Once there, he barged into a waiting room full of people and said to the receptionist, ''I have to talk to Kelly immediately.''

''She's with a patient. If you'll have a seat—''

''Kelly!'' he yelled past her. Not waiting for an answer, he flung open the door and went down the hall shouting, ''Kelly!''

The receptionist ran after him. ''Mr. Outlaw! Wait!''

''Kelly!''

One of the doors flew open, and Kelly stepped out. ''What in the world is—''

He bear-hugged her and swung her around. "I'm going to be a professor!"

"Cole Outlaw! Put me down. Have you lost your mind?"

He laughed and kissed her. "Yes. The moment I met you."

"Cole, *shhhh*," she whispered. "I have patients—"

"They won't care. They love you. I love you. I have fantastic news, darlin'. John Becker just called and offered me a job teaching at the college in Travis Lake, and I'm going to accept. Now we can get married and live here. Come on," he said, grabbing her hand. "Let's go over to the courthouse and get Frank to marry us right now."

"No!" She yanked her hand from his.

"No? I thought you loved me."

"I do love you, but I'm not going to marry you right now. That's totally ridiculous."

"If not now, when?" he asked.

"Let's talk later," she whispered.

"Let's talk now." He didn't whisper. "Set a date."

"How about next weekend?"

"You heard that," he said to Reba Conroy, who'd stuck her head out of one of the patient rooms. "It's a deal," he said to Kelly. "I've got witnesses."

He took her in his arms and kissed her with all the love that was in his heart. He'd come back to Naconiche to heal his body and found Kelly, who had healed his soul.

"I love you, Dr. Martin."

The nurses and patients all burst into enthusiastic applause, and he kissed her again.

Epilogue

Kelly was sitting in front of the mirror putting on her makeup when Cole bent down and kissed her cheek.

"Hello, there, Dr. Outlaw," she said.

"Hello, yourself, Dr. Martin-Outlaw. Do I have time to change? Red here spit up on me."

"If you hurry. And don't call her Red. Call her Elizabeth. Where have you two been, anyhow?"

"We've been out doing some last minute Christmas shopping."

"For what?"

"You'll have to ask her," he said, winking at his daughter who gurgled at him. "I'm sworn to secrecy." He set the carrier on the floor beside Kelly and started unbuttoning his shirt. "Have you talked to your folks?"

"Yes, they called a few minutes ago. They adore the islands."

Her parents had decided to go on a cruise over the holidays, and Kelly had encouraged them. She sort of wanted to spend Elizabeth's first Christmas alone with her husband and daughter. Of course, three months was too young to know about Santa, but they had bought far too many gifts anyhow. Tonight they were going over to Frank and Carrie's house for the Outlaw party, but tomorrow they could sleep in. It would probably be the last Christmas that they would be able to.

"Does Elizabeth need changing?" she asked.

"I don't know," Cole said as he came out of the closet pulling down his sweater. "I'll check."

Cole was a wonderful father. He adored their daughter and spoiled her rotten. He had arranged to teach afternoon and evening classes for the fall semester so that he could be with Elizabeth in the mornings when Kelly saw patients.

His wounds had healed. Only occasionally, when he was very tired, was there any sign of a limp.

"She's dry," he said. "Ready to go?"

"All set. If you'll get her, I'll get the diaper bag and the casserole."

"Tuna?"

"Lord, no. Sweet potato. Gladys has gone to visit her niece."

They loaded up the SUV and drove out to the country.

Carrie and Frank, who had married in June, had spent a week decorating again. Santa waved from his sleigh pulled by the log reindeer, and lights twinkled from the eaves and trees. Pine and holly swags adorned the porch.

Carrie waited at the door, beaming. "Come in," she said, touching her cheek to Kelly's, then to Cole's. "Merry Christmas."

Kelly knew the reason for Carrie's glow. She was pregnant. She and Frank would be making the announcement to the family tonight. What was funny was that J.J. and Mary Beth would be making the same announcement. Neither couple knew about the other, and she hadn't mentioned it to Cole...or to anyone.

She hugged Nonie and Wes on the way to the kitchen with the casserole. They, along with the twins, were on their way to commandeer the baby. She stopped by the bar and poured a glass of wine for Cole and one for herself. She found him in the den talking with Belle and Matt Carson, her fiancé.

"Are you sorry you left HPD, Big Buzzer?" Belle asked Cole.

"Lord, no. I love teaching. I can't believe that it took me so long to figure out that it's what I do best. Are you sorry you left the FBI, Ding?"

"Nope." She hooked her arm through Matt's. "Not one bit. And we have an announcement to make at dinner."

"What?"

Belle smiled. "You'll have to wait, Big Buzzer."

"Ho! Ho! Ho!" J.J. said as he and Mary Beth came in carrying foil-wrapped platters. "Merry Christmas!"

Katy trailed behind carrying a small wrapped dish. "We have turkey and ham," she said. "And I have cranberry sauce."

"And I have about twelve dozen rolls," Sam said as he came in holding up two baskets.

"Which I'm sure that you made with your own two hands," Frank said, laughing.

"No, I did," said Julie, the blonde beside him.

Sam winked down at her. "I'm smart. I picked out one who could cook."

"I'm starving," Jimmy said.

"Me, too," Janey said.

"Me, three," Katy said.

"Nobody in this family ever starves," Wes Outlaw said. "Let's eat."

A smaller table was added for the children, but everybody else managed to squeeze around the big table in the dining room. After the prayer, Frank rose and dinged on his glass.

"Carrie and I have an announcement to make. We're going to have an addition to our family next summer."

"You buying another horse?" Sam asked.

J.J. thumped Sam's head and stood. "No, bonehead. Sounds like they're having a baby. Congratulations. So are we."

Everyone beamed and clapped and murmured.

Belle stood. "Matt and I have an announcement as well."

"When is yours due?" Sam asked.

J.J. thumped him again, but Belle only laughed. "Not for a couple of years. But we are getting married this Sunday, here. Frank is performing the ceremony and you're all invited."

There was more murmuring and smiling and clapping.

Sam rose. "I guess that this is as good a time as any to announce that I asked Julie to marry me, and she's said yes."

"Way to go!" some said amid more clapping.

J.J. looked at Cole. "You have any announcement to make?"

Cole stood, and grinned down at Kelly in that way that still made her heart flutter. "Not yet. We've had our quota of announcements for the year, but I would like to propose a toast." He raised his glass. "To all the Outlaws and in-laws and to those who are joining our clan. May the years ahead be filled with peace and joy and love. Merry Christmas."

"Hear! Hear!"

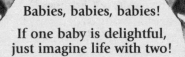
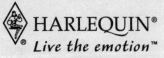

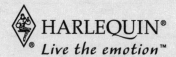

If you enjoyed what you just read,
then we've got an offer you can't resist!

Take 2 bestselling
love stories FREE!
Plus get a FREE surprise gift!

Clip this page and mail it to Harlequin Reader Service®

IN U.S.A.
3010 Walden Ave.
P.O. Box 1867
Buffalo, N.Y. 14240-1867

IN CANADA
P.O. Box 609
Fort Erie, Ontario
L2A 5X3

YES! Please send me 2 free Harlequin American Romance® novels and my free surprise gift. After receiving them, if I don't wish to receive anymore, I can return the shipping statement marked cancel. If I don't cancel, I will receive 4 brand-new novels every month, before they're available in stores! In the U.S.A., bill me at the bargain price of $4.24 plus 25¢ shipping & handling per book and applicable sales tax, if any*. In Canada, bill me at the bargain price of $4.99 plus 25¢ shipping & handling per book and applicable taxes**. That's the complete price and a savings of at least 10% off the cover prices—what a great deal! I understand that accepting the 2 free books and gift places me under no obligation ever to buy any books. I can always return a shipment and cancel at any time. Even if I never buy another book from Harlequin, the 2 free books and gift are mine to keep forever.

154 HDN DZ7S
354 HDN DZ7T

Name	(PLEASE PRINT)
Address	Apt.#
City	State/Prov. Zip/Postal Code

* Terms and prices subject to change without notice. Sales tax applicable in N.Y.
** Canadian residents will be charged applicable provincial taxes and GST.
   All orders subject to approval. Offer limited to one per household and not valid to
   current Harlequin American Romance® subscribers.
   ® are registered trademarks owned and used by the trademark owner and or its licensee.

AMER04   ©2004 Harlequin Enterprises Limited

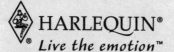

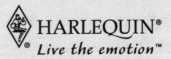